UNFINISHED BUSINESS

UNFINISHED BUSINESS

TIM SUSMAN

Unfinished Business
Production copyright Argyll Productions © 2022
Text copyright © Tim Susman 2022
Published by Argyll Productions
Dallas, Texas
www.argyllproductions.com

Cover design by Damonza.com
Interior design by Argyll Productions

ISBN 978-1-61450-559-4

First Edition Trade Paperback

To everyone who has ever wanted a werewolf

To everyone who has ever counted a bee yield

CHAPTER 1
AN EASY JOB

The silver detector blared as I walked through the security gate into Wolftown Chicago, so I got my PI license out before the guard could go from surprised to suspicious. Most of the guards here knew me, but this kid was new, probably part of the recent haul from the Paranormal Guard recruitment drives in Chicago proper.

He said my name out loud as he squinted at the license. "Jae...Kim?"

"That's right," I said. "I have a silver implant. Can't remove it." I tapped my collarbone. "It's right behind here. And that gun and silver bullets are mine, too."

"Silver implant." He kept reading the license. "They told us those don't work."

"They can be a mild deterrent." I'd found it wasn't worth telling people that I had a paranoid mother, and that I'd talked her down from wearing a silver choker every time I went into Wolftown. At least the implant was discreet and the very minor surgery had been basically an afternoon.

"Okay, sir. Have a good...uh." In the process of handing me my phone and license back, he froze, staring over my shoulder.

"Oh," I said, not having to turn to know what had appeared behind me. "That's Sergei. He's with me."

"I have no silver on me," rumbled the seven-foot tall Russian ghost bear.

The guard swallowed and turned his head without taking his eyes off Sergei. "I need a ghost check! Ghost check!"

"It is profiling," Sergei grumbled once we were past the security gate. He'd gone invisible again once outside the confines of the checkpoint, even though a berserker in full bear form wouldn't raise eyebrows (bushy or otherwise) in most areas of Wolftown. Nobody could tell he was a ghost by sight unless he floated or went translucent but I preferred he stay out of sight while I was working unless I was trying to intimidate someone. "All ghost are suspicious. What have I done? Why must I be subjected to humiliation? Poking and staring, never trusting."

"I don't trust you," I pointed out, fiddling with the binding ring on my finger. The spell on the gates that kept unbound ghosts out of Wolftown had been known to scramble binding spells occasionally, and the Paranormal Guard always denied responsibility. "And unbound ghosts do some fucked-up shit."

"Jae, you know so little of ghosts." He heaved a deep sigh right next to my ear. "If you do not trust me then perhaps you should let me go. I will trouble you no further."

"Get over your dead wife and you can release yourself."

"You do not understand true love," he said, mournful as only Russians can be. "At least, you do not appreciate it—"

"Besides," I cut in to head off that argument, "I need you."

2

"How touching."

"Without you, my job would be harder."

"Hmph," he growled.

We stepped out of the dank concrete tunnel and onto Kennelly Plaza, the big public square that welcomed tourists, residents, and the occasional visiting professional with their ghost partners to Wolftown.

Chicago's Wolftown is the second oldest in the country, but only the fifth-largest since Wolftown Seattle expanded a few years ago. Internationally there are walled neighborhoods and cities where the werewolves and vampires and other extrahuman creatures ("extras") can live, but they don't call them Wolftowns. That name was coined, the Internet says, by Bo Washington, a columnist for the New York Times back in 1952 when the New York Wolftown was being built, and it stuck.

I always felt like stepping into Wolftown was going back in time. There's no skyscrapers here, or even buildings that look like they might grow up to be skyscrapers one day. The tallest building in Wolftown Chicago is a fifteen-story apartment tower which stands over five smaller buildings like a proud parent. Meanwhile, a small complex of high-rise condos just outside the walls flashes smug blue glass at the extras here, and from certain spots you can see over the walls to the giant office buildings of the Loop.

But then there's modern green spaces for the werewolves and big windowless warehouse lofts for the vampires. Those two general types make up the majority of the extras here and have generally taken over the city planning even though Wolftown Chicago has the second-greatest diversity of kinds of extras, after Wolftown L.A. There are about thirty different kinds in the world depending on who you ask. For example, are the Adze and Sasabonsam and Obayifo all counted as vampires like the European vampires? They all drink blood and can change shape, but Euro vampires mostly just become bats; the Sasabonsam have iron teeth and can also become bats; the Obayifo have glowing butts (really) and a strict pack structure and can throw their spirits out of their body into another person or animal; the Adze turn into giant fireflies and can also throw their spirits. I think those are pretty different, but some people don't look past "drink blood, change shape," so they all get lumped together, or maybe classified as "European vampires and African vampires."

Likewise, there are three different kinds of nine-tailed fox spirit: kitsune, from Japan; huli jing, from China, and kumiho, from Korea. They have different cultures but a lot of people just go "Asian foxes" and leave it at that. In Wolftown Chicago, as it happens, there's a pretty large kumiho community and I know a lot of the people there, so I skirted the tourist-trap shops around Kennelly Plaza on my way to the two-block Koreatown.

The stores with big gaudy signs blaring "Garlic and Wolfs-bane Bunches $2" and "Get Your Picture With a Werewolf $5" and "Wolftown T-shirts $15" had collected groups of tourists, not to mention the stands selling hundreds of little bronze and plaster sculptures of giant movie werewolves standing in a generic walled city or movie vampires with bloodshot eyes and fangs. The vendors here mostly shift to fully human because the tourists don't feel as comfortable buying even Wolftown souvenirs from bipedal shirtless fur-covered people with a wolf head, clawed paw-hands, and a tail. More fool them.

Most of the locals wandering around Kennelly Plaza also stay in full human form for that reason, but every so often you'll get one like this guy who was coming toward me with a Bears hat between his brown pointed ears, a wide grin on his wolf's muzzle, wearing nothing else but loose athletic shorts so that his ivory chest fur and the brown-grey fur on the rest of his body was on full display. He sauntered onto the plaza and stopped as soon as one of the tourists aimed a phone at him, holding up two fingers in the "peace" sign.

Soon enough there were twenty tourists all clustered around taking pictures. "Show-off," muttered Sergei invisibly beside me.

"Leave him alone." I glanced back at the wolf, posing with one of the tourists. He kept his fingers away from her ostentatious silver necklace that I was sure hid a cross below the dress's neckline. "He's trying to be an ambassador."

The bear chuckled in my ear. "Plus he has cute butt, no?"

"I wasn't looking."

"Jae. I see what you see."

Another old argument I wasn't going to win. We turned down Alvarez, where the tourist shops thinned out and gave way to the places locals shopped: grocery stores, grooming salons, cafes. Down some of the darker alleys, out of my sight but not my knowledge, were legal sex shops where tourists could spice up their sex lives.

Sergei, as he often did, followed the same train of thought. "There is no chance this Mister MacArthur is getting sex?" he asked, a touch wistfully.

"Not this time." More of the locals on this street walked around as half-wolves, like the one who'd posed for the tourists. A couple blocks farther in, the only people walking around looking human would be the pale vampires, or maybe a naga if they were in a hurry.

"Is worth checking, no?"

"If he's not in the first five places on our list, then yes, you can check the local sex shops."

Surrounded by extras unafraid to show their fangs and tails, I got the real feeling of Wolftown: an alien world where I moved easily but still didn't belong. As an army liaison and later a PI, I'd cultivated the skill of reading expressions and body language in humans and then had to learn it all over again for extras. Most people didn't bother; they just saw a bunch of wolf- and fox- and bear-headed people roaming around with the odd vampire thrown in. I could look at the wolf couple deep in conversation across the street and tell that the one with flat-back ears and arched tail was reprimanding the other, whose tucked tail said they knew they'd done something wrong.

If I were closer, and had a wolf's nose and a lifetime of experience, I'd be able to tell a lot more about them. Part of the reason they spent their lives in animal-shifted form was to teach themselves to sense the world through their animal ears, eyes, and noses. Their tongue and vocal cords weren't exactly the same, but by an adult age most of them had mastered the art of shifting enough to be able to talk in a close approximation of their human voice (and to be able to see colors too).

That said, if you worked with someone in your human office and then ran across them in their wolf-shifted form in Wolftown, very likely you wouldn't recognize their voice. That's one case where natural circumstances intersect with safe practices. For a while in the seventies there was a "Hire Werewolves" initiative and then there was a panic about how to tell a werewolf (the answer: you can tell a werewolf if they tell you, "I'm a werewolf," and otherwise it's none of your damn business). A bunch of disgusting companies made bank on silver paper clips for a while. Now there are disclosure requirements, and every decade or so some conservative shithead brings up mandatory registration, but so far it hasn't gone anywhere.

As we turned from Alvarez onto MacArthur, the street signs featured Korean characters. I could read them, but my grasp of the language was tenuous. Back in the 80s when I grew up, Mom and Dad believed that if they raised me to speak Korean at home, I'd have an accent that would make me stand out at school, so we spoke English in the house. In some ways it made things easier, although when I got to college I'd make several friends who spoke both English and their parents' native language fluently, which gave me a bit of a complex about it. Fifteen years after I graduated, now everyone values their family's culture of origin. I've taken a couple Korean lessons but I'm still not better than the average college student.

Pete, the kumiho who runs Seoul Food Cafe, was in her fox form when I came in, nine golden-orange tails swishing behind her in rhythm to the Alicia Keys song on the radio (Pete introduced me to Alicia Keys' music; I still favor grunge-alternative, though Sergei insists on some speed metal breaks). She looked up, saw me, and her narrow vulpine muzzle grew a huge toothy smile. "Jae!"

In the time it took me to say, "Hey, Pete. Coffee, please," her large fox's ears and sharp muzzle withdrew into her head. That golden-orange fur smoothed into human skin, and the clawed paws that had been wiping down the counter changed to hands with iridescent black nail polish. The tails stayed, though. Pete liked her tails.

"Sure thing," she said. "We got a dark roast from Sumatra if you wanna try it, or we got your usual dark."

Sumatra dark, Sergei nudged me.

"The Sumatran will be great." I took out a five and dropped it on the counter, then went to a table near the big front window. The cafe wasn't too full; a fox on her laptop in one corner and a pair of foxes having a hushed (to me; not to them) conversation over kimchi chicken and waffles.

All right, I told Sergei. *Coffee's on the way. Go find this guy.*

I tell you, he is in sex shop.

7

Doesn't fit his profile, but go through our list and see if you spot him anywhere.

He grumbled but quieted as he went off to investigate the library, the two hotels, the B&B, and the youth hostel. Someone trying to avoid a summons in Wolftown usually went to those places, and our Robert MacArthur, a middle-aged VP of a financial services firm who was trying to avoid going to court in the divorce suit his wife was bringing, probably thought he could hide out here while his lawyers worked on a countersuit or motions or whatever. I didn't know the particulars of the legal system; what I knew was that a surprising number of people thought that they could avoid a lawsuit forever if they just never got served a summons. I'd been a PI for almost four years and I'd yet to take more than a week to find and serve someone. Most cases took less than two days.

Pete brought my coffee and change over and plopped down in the seat across from mine, letting her tails drape elegantly down so the tips barely brushed the floor. Her eyes remained the unsettling slit-pupiled amber of a fox. "Who's got the mighty Kim on their trail today?"

The coffee smelled rich and nutty, with light chocolatey overtones, and also almost burned my nose from an inch away. I set it back down. For her customers with more sensitive noses, Pete would dilute the original with water or milk, but to us poor impaired humans, she served the unadulterated stuff. "Some d-bag from high finance," I said. "Playing shitty games with his soon-to-be ex-wife."

"Straight people." She stuck out her tongue.

"Tell me about it. Although I'm getting more calls about cheating gays and lesbians now that marriage is legal for us."

Pete cocked her head. "Is there such a thing as a cheating gay? Don't you all just sleep with whoever?"

"Ha ha," I said. "Everybody sleeps with whoever these days."

Not true, Sergei said into my head.

Get to work, I told him.

"But people still seem worried about cheating." Pete shook her head.

"If you read something other than TMZ once in a while, you wouldn't think that. Try the Guardian. Even CNN manages to have actual news on it once in a while."

She stuck her tongue out at me. "I like my stories." She leaned forward. "I know your whole thing about cheating but if Jenny Levinson called you and asked you to follow Bruce Rutledge, you'd do it, right?"

"I don't know who either of those people are, so I'm gonna say no."

"Oh, you know Bruce Rutledge." She rattled off the titles of three movies, the last of which I'd seen. "That one. He was the bad guy."

"Okay, I guess I do know him, but still no."

"Jae, he's gay. He's cheating on her with the assistant director on *How We Saved the Moon*."

"I don't buy it. He's a rich white guy. If he were gay, he'd be out."

She snorted. "Like it's so easy. What about—"

The door to the cafe opened, catching both our attention. A werewolf walked in, shirtless and in loose shorts. His tail swung from side to side as he surveyed the cafe, and then he came over to our table.

A lot of wolves have green eyes and black-tipped ears, but not a lot of wolves have a reflex to check out a room when they enter it, looking for alternate exits and possible threats. I didn't recognize him specifically, but I knew where he knew me from the minute his eyes met mine, and I knew that keeping his ears up meant that he was pleased to see me, so I relaxed. "Hey," I said.

"Hi. Sergeant Kim, right?" He had a low gruff voice even for a wolf, and the light Eastern European accent confirmed my guess.

"That's right."

His posture relaxed and he smiled. "It's good to see you again. I know you probably don't recognize me. My name's Alan, but it was Erlin when you knew me."

"Kosovo," I said, and reached a hand up. His paw met it, and we shook. "Join us?"

"You can have my chair." Pete got up. "I've got cookies to put in the oven and I don't need to hear war talk."

"Oh, it's not—" But she was already walking away, tails fanning out behind her. She raised one hand that turned into a dark brown fox paw.

So Alan sat down across from me. His ears flicked back (self-consciously at having made Pete leave, I guessed) and then came forward again. "I was one of the kids from Viti. You, uh, you gave me some of your food."

I'd done that for a lot of kids. We weren't supposed to, but when the aid packages were delayed, it was hard not to. "I remember Viti," I said, and then to be scrupulously honest, "I don't remember you specifically, but I'm glad you're doing okay."

"Yeah." His tail swept the floor. "A bunch of us got together a couple months ago, and some of the officers came to the reunion. It was nice." He didn't ask why I wasn't there, which meant he knew. "But anyway, I run warrants here now for Chicago PD sometimes, I mean, for the last six months, and I got one this morning for this guy, MacArthur."

My eyes widened, and he read the look, nodding. "Yeah, the same one. I called his wife and she told me she'd hired a detective to go into Wolftown but wouldn't say who even when I guessed your name. I tried calling, but..."

"I don't bring my work number on jobs," I said. "How'd you find me?"

"Oh, uh, I've seen you around here before. At least, I was pretty sure it was you. The scent was—ah, I never had a reason to come say hi."

"You don't need a reason." I gave him my most reassuring smile, letting him know I wasn't offended that he'd sniffed me out. Some people could be touchy about that. "Congrats on the job. How long did it take you to get the certification?"

He wiggled his paw in the "so-so" gesture. "About a month. I'm good with the law part but I failed marksmanship twice."

"If you're only gonna be good at one thing, the law's the one." I tipped back some of the coffee, now drinkable. "If you miss a shot, you could die, but if you fuck up the law, your life could be really ruined."

He smiled at the joke and nodded with some vigor. "Oh, I know. My brother quizzed me every night for a month and wouldn't let me take the test until I got all his questions right."

"So what does the CPD want with MacArthur?" I asked.

"The warrant says 'physical threats and erratic behavior.' The cop I talked to said something about him getting drunk at his office, but his wife said it was her office, that he quit his job. She also said he was selling their house without her permission or something. Anyway I guess he had a gun and he waved it around, so they reported him, but he ran in here."

"What a winner." I was glad my gun was loaded. I hated using it, and I'd rarely had to fire it. In this case, though, if the guy had a gun, it was best if I had one too. The silver bullets remained unloaded; MacArthur wasn't an extra.

Alan flicked his ears and looked away: nervousness. "So, uh," he said, "would you want to work together on this?"

Say yes, Sergei rumbled.

"That's fine," I said. "For this one time. I don't care if you arrest him as long as I get to serve the warrant."

"Oh, good." He smiled and I heard the brush of his tail wagging again. "Where should we start?"

"My partner's already looking," I said.

"Your, uh..." He took out a phone and tapped it with his claws, then scrolled up. I could just see from the angle that he was looking at my website. "Oh! You have a ghost. I missed that. How do you get a ghost partner? Put 'help wanted' signs up on haunted houses?"

"Heh." I gave his joke the same smile he'd given mine. "You buy one. But it's a little more involved than that. You have to bind the ghost with a spell and an object," I held up my hand with the ring on it, "and if you screw up the spell, the ghost can possess you and kill you."

His ears went back. "If the ghost would kill you, why do you want them as a partner?"

"No," I said, "it's just before they're bound that they'll kill you. And that's rare. See, being a ghost puts you in something like a manic anxiety spiral—like a form of PTSD where your trigger is anyone living."

"Shit," Alan said.

"Yep. They're prone to more and more destructive behavior the longer they're unbound. But the spell gives them an anchor so they're more like they were in life. Like, Sergei was pretty dangerous when he was unbound, but now even though he jokes about wanting to be set free, he's a good friend." I would've said "my best friend" if that wouldn't make me seem really sad. "And a great partner."

Alan digested that. "Oh. Cool. So he's going around to...?"

"A few places." The thought about the silver bullets came back to me: MacArthur wasn't an extra. Yet. "But...shit, we hadn't known about him quitting his job and selling the house. I thought he was just hiding out here like people do, but what if he wasn't running *away* from something? What if he was running *to*..."

Alan's muzzle twisted and his ears flattened back. Disgust, I thought. "Ah, shit," he said.

Sergei, I said. *Check the bite houses.*

Alan got up quickly. I took another swallow of the coffee and stood at the same time. "Where's the nearest place?" I asked.

He paused with one paw on the chair back. "They change around so often. I don't know this part of town."

"He might not even be in this part of town." I knew of a couple bite houses, but Alan was right, they did change around all the time, and I wanted to see what someone just searching on the Internet would find if he looked now. I took out my phone to check and Alan did the same.

From behind the counter, Pete called, "What's going on?"

Most of the searches for "bite house wolftown chicago" turned up the same standard Wikipedia text about bite houses and how in every state that has a Wolftown you need to pass a mental and psychiatric examination and then wait a month before you can get a legal transformation to become a were-creature of whatever sort. Most involve bites, but some have other rituals. Werewolves are one of the easiest: just get a werewolf chewing some wolfsbane to bite you, and the saliva and herb mix together to turn you. Wolfsbane gets werewolves kinda drunk, so it's common in Wolftowns even though it's technically illegal. Of course, wherever there are laws, there are people willing to break them for a price.

"We think this guy might be at a bite house," I told her.

Her long, sharp muzzle twisted. "Gross. There's one like two blocks that way." She pointed directly out the window. "Sketchy guys stop in here every couple weeks and ask for directions."

I told Sergei and he headed there immediately. "Thanks, Pete," I said. "Maybe Alan here can get them shut down."

Alan's ears went back. "I'm only supposed to execute my warrant," he said, holding the door for me.

"You can report the house to the police. Register a complaint and that'll start things moving."

"Okay." The ears came back up as we got out onto the sidewalk. Having Alan at my side made me stand out less to the residents of Wolftown; we got fewer stares even though we hurried around people in the street.

He is not here, Sergei told me, and I grabbed Alan's arm to bring him to a stop.

Check the two we know about, I told Sergei, and to the wolf beside me, I said, "He's not at that one."

Alan's nostrils flared and he swung his head back and forth. "He's been in Wolftown for a couple hours. He could've been and gone already."

"Even at the bite houses, they make you wait an hour to make sure they don't have to drop you at a hospital," I said. "If that's where he went, then he's probably still there."

"I don't know anything about them," Alan said as we took off in the direction of the closest one. Whether he was protesting because he didn't want me to think badly of him or excusing his ignorance, I believed him.

Chicago Wolftown is just a touch over two square miles, so you can walk from one end of it to the other in half an hour. Like all the Wolftowns, there's no cars here, although there are rental bikes and scooters, enough that Alan and I could each grab a bike and pedal to our destination, him carefully keeping his tail out of the way of the back wheel.

Few enough people use the scooters and bikes that Alan and I had to use our horns liberally as we raced across town. The glamorous life of a private eye: riding a bike across town honking my horn to intercept a guy before he lets a werewolf bite him. Mike Hammer never rides bikes in his movies.

I have found him, Sergei told me as we turned onto Prizren Avenue, just three blocks from the location.

Is he—?

He was ready to enter room where the biting takes place. I have discouraged it.

I got a brief chuckle out of imagining how that had gone down, and then I saw Robert MacArthur, unmistakable in his disheveled collared shirt, khakis, and human skin. He stared wildly both ways down the street, started running toward me and Alan, and then saw us and froze.

We were the only ones on bikes and we were both pedaling pretty fast toward him, so I guess it wasn't too hard to figure out. He turned and dashed the other way, about as fast as you'd expect a middle-aged finance guy to run. We would have caught up to him easily except that he ran down an alley and climbed onto a large dumpster. While we were dismounting our bikes, he leapt for the nearest fire escape.

I seriously thought he wouldn't make it, and my first reaction was, at least we won't have to chase him anymore. But his fingers caught a railing and he pulled himself up just ahead of Alan, who swiped at his ankle and missed it by inches.

For someone who clearly had taken all his notes on running away from formulaic action movies, this guy was doing a credible job of it. I mean, there was a restaurant's service entrance right down the alley; there was a crowded grocery store a little farther down. And a quarter mile behind us were a bunch of tourist groups. Sergei would have tracked him into any of those places, but still, if you were trying to avoid pursuit in Wolftown and you didn't look like a wolf, they made a lot more sense than trying to climb up to the roof of a building. And yet, there he was, climbing the fire escape faster than I would have thought possible.

"Where is he going?" Alan came back over to stand beside me and looked up, scratching behind one ear.

"The roof, probably. I guess he thinks he's going to run across rooftops like Spider-Man or something."

The wolf gave me a look. "Does this happen a lot?"

"Not really. Once I had a guy jump out of a window to avoid me."

"Oh shit. A high window?"

"Four stories, but there was an awning under it."

The guy above us had climbed that high now, with one to go before he made it to the roof. Alan folded his arms, keeping an eye on our fugitive. "Huh. So he was okay?"

"Oh, no. Those awnings are canvas, but the supports aren't that strong. It snapped off the side of the building and he broke both his legs on the sidewalk."

"Ouch." He nodded up. "You think he's gonna jump?"

"If he can find an awning. You want to go up after him and I'll shadow him on the ground? I think you're faster on foot."

Alan flashed a smile. "Oh, yeah, that sounds great."

He took off for the fire escape and got onto it impressively, leaping with a running start onto the garbage bin and springing to the metal lattice from there. I had a distracted moment thinking about the musculature of a werewolf and then I called after him, "I'll have Sergei contact you if I find anything."

The wolf shot me a thumbs-up as he vaulted up the metal

stairs two at a time. MacArthur had by this time disappeared onto the roof, but Sergei had ghost eyes on him.

He is looking around roof. Now he runs across many buildings and goes to edge to see if he can jump. Also this is not good time for flirting.

Which edge? I asked back. *Also, I wasn't flirting.*

Ha. Opposite side of building from you.

Anyway, you keep telling me to meet someone, I said, and left the alley to walk around the front of the building.

And you always say, business first. Handsome wolf is on roof now. MacArthur looks frightened. I think he may jump.

Scare him away from the edge, I said, hurrying past six five-story apartment buildings clustered close together. I hooked a right at the end of that block and onto Sirius Street, which was definitely too wide for MacArthur to jump over, but not so wide that he might not try.

A high-pitched scream came from above me. I looked up and saw the edge of Sergei's seven-foot bear body on the roof. It moved out of my sight, onto the roof, and the scream came again.

Don't kill him, I said.

Pah. He is crying. Handsome wolf is almost here.

You're not helping by calling him handsome, I said.

You do not think he is handsome?

That's—not the point.

Sergei didn't respond for a few seconds. I paced on the street, wondering what was happening, and then I saw through Sergei's eyes.

Alan knelt beside a prone MacArthur, who was staring directly at Sergei and babbling. "There was a bear, a huge bear, right in front of me, I swear it."

"Sure, sure," Alan said. Sergei's view shifted to a low angle, looking up at Alan's head, his muzzle catching the sunlight so the fur appeared warm and soft and his eyes shone. I could see his whiskers and the short fur on his ears.

Now is time for flirting, Sergei told me.

"Ask Alan if he needs help getting MacArthur down," I told Sergei. "And don't ask him anything else."

The bear's only response as my vision snapped back to my own body was a theatrical sigh.

Alan did not need help getting MacArthur down. He appeared at the front of the apartment building with the man slung over his shoulder like a sack of sad, broken toys and sat him down on the stoop. By this time, MacArthur had recovered some of his poise. "You can't just walk up and arrest me," he said. "What about due process? I've got a lawyer."

"And I've got a warrant," Alan growled, producing the paper from a pocket of his shorts. He waved it in front of MacArthur, who shied away as if the paper smelled. Maybe it did; it had been in a wolf's pocket for a while. "I'm authorized to use force, especially since you had that gun on you."

My hand went to my own gun. "He was armed?"

"I left it on the roof." Alan grabbed MacArthur by the arm. "I'll come back and get it after I hand him over."

"I can go up." The apartment door hadn't fully closed, so I'd be able to get to the roof easily. "It's no trouble. I'll bring it to you at Kennelly."

"Sure, okay," Alan said. "You know it's not a big deal, though, right? It's not—unh, come on—loaded with silver." MacArthur was resisting, trying to make himself heavier, refusing to put his feet under him.

"I know. I just don't like leaving loose ends."

"Fair enough." He yanked MacArthur to his feet and addressed him. "Asshole, if you want I can carry you all the way there and dump you in front of the cops like a little baby. You want that?"

Sulkily, the asshole stood. "You don't have to grab me so hard."

"I kinda think I do," Alan said. "You made me climb a fire escape and chase you across a roof. Oh, and Sergeant Kim here has something for you too."

I pulled the papers out of my shoulder bag. "Here. Whenever the CPD lets you go, you're being summoned to court."

He looked angrier than when Alan had tossed him to the ground. "What? That bitch, she sent someone into Wolftown? Fuck her, and fuck you, and fuck you too!" This last was to Alan.

"All right, champ, that's enough. You don't talk to Sergeant Kim like that." Alan grabbed the guy by the collar of his expensive-looking shirt and with his other paw took the papers I was holding out and stuffed them down the front of the shirt. "There. You been served. Let's go."

"I have to take the papers in my hand!" he yelled, loudly and incorrectly. "I'm a citizen of the city of Chicago! You can't do this to a human!"

He continued to invent imaginary ways out of the predicament he'd gotten himself into, shouting them for everyone to hear as Alan half-dragged him down the street.

I shook my head and slipped into the apartment building. The smell of wolf surrounded me, wrapped around my shoulders and tickled my memory. I walked through both the smell and the memory to the stairs, five stories of them. Three stories up, the wall bore what looked like a fresh scar, a gleaming patch of white plaster in the dull brown paint. I estimated Alan's height, thought about the way he'd been carrying

MacArthur. Yep, that was about where a petulant heel would connect with the wall.

Up on the roof, Sergei became visible near the gun so I wouldn't have to search. "Thanks," I said, taking a cloth from my pocket to pick it up.

"Very clever of you."

"What," I said, "the cloth? Thanks, but Sam Spade pioneered that one. Probably got it from the Continental Op."

"I mean this trick. It is like this thing you call the 'leave-behind,' no? You tell him you will get gun so you may see him again."

"Jesus, Sergei, let it go," I said. "I'm not into him."

"Pity. He is into you."

"He's not." We were near the edge of the roof. I looked over at the wolves walking up and down the street, tails wagging and hanging behind them, ears perking and flicking at each other.

"We call it 'love of puppy' in Russian army."

I weighed the cloth-wrapped gun, and something rattled. Not a sound that anyone who knew anything about guns would trust. "You did not, you called it something probably eighteen words long referencing a crocus blossom in the midst of a snowpack that blooms during the first morning after a long night of grief. And anyway, if he is 'into me,' like you say, it's just misplaced, paternal, um, something or another. I knew him when he was literally a puppy. Well, late teens."

Sergei laughed. "So I am not wrong. Love of puppy."

"It's a crush left over from his adolescence."

"Any way you can arrive at love is worthwhile."

"How do you know it will arrive at love?"

"How do you know it will not?"

I didn't answer, just put the gun into my bag and headed for the door. Sergei went invisible and silent but he spoke again as I exited the building. "Jae, move forward or go back. To stop in the middle of winter is to die."

"It's springtime, in case you hadn't noticed," I said, "and I don't mix work and pleasure anyway, and when has your nagging me ever made things better?"

"Six months ago," he said. "Very enjoyable night. You always search for love and not simply pleasure."

"And then like three weeks of awkward messaging after. You remember that too?"

"Of course. I tell you to respond. You say no, you find reasons why not."

"That guy wasn't right. One good night is not the only requirement for a lifetime together. Sometimes you can get years down the road believing that all these problems will work themselves out, but they won't."

I got a curious glance from a wolf—human talking to himself in the middle of Wolftown couldn't be something he saw every day, and my short-cropped black hair made it obvious I wasn't wearing a Bluetooth earpiece. But I didn't smell too different from what he was expecting, I guess, so he walked on by. Sergei kept his voice down. "Some things become difficult because you make them difficult."

Like beats of an old record, this argument. "And some things are difficult because they're difficult."

"You talk to me of difficult?"

"Here we go." I rolled my eyes pre-emptively.

"How many nights have you spent sleeping on hard ground under skin of bear?"

"That was your skin, idiot."

"How many nights do you search Russian forest for scraps of reindeer?"

"Does the Kosovo forest count?"

There was no stopping a Russian when he got talking

about his homeland, even when he was complaining about it. "This thing you call 'winter' here in Chicago, this is balmy spring day in Russia. I will tell you of walking on ice of river for miles to approach rebel camp without being seen. You do not know how white snow can be until blood splashes red on it. My claws tore great rents through the rebels."

"They broke and fled before you into the snow," I said. "Some of them froze to death and you found them the next day and feasted on their bodies."

"Hmph."

"And now you sneak around like a spy and there is no glory in what we do," I finished. "This is a little off topic, don't you think?"

"Russia always on topic."

I turned onto Alvarez and headed for Kennelly. "Live in the present."

"I will if you will."

In the next block, tourists walked around gawking at the buildings and the residents, so I stood out less. "I'm going to give him the gun," I said, "and that's it. I'm not going to ask for his number or anything."

In the thicker crowd, Sergei chose not to speak aloud. *If you insist.*

Back in Kennelly Plaza, the show-off wolf was gone but a vampire dressed in a black cape was performing for a crowd of star-struck tourists. I hurried to the security tunnel and told security I was delivering some evidence to the warrant officer. They took me through a side door to where Alan was thumbing through his phone beside a sulky MacArthur.

I assumed it was Alan, anyway; he was wearing the same loose shorts but he'd shifted to his human form, with dark unkempt hair and brown eyes, a prominent nose over a half-grin, and a reasonably good-looking chest and stomach. When he looked up, his eyes lit up the same way, and in a different voice he said, "Sergeant Kim! It's Alan."

"I guessed." I hid a smile as I handed over the gun. If he had a tail it would be wagging.

"Hey, thanks." He took the gun and tucked it under an arm. "You mind if we talk outside for a minute?"

"Careful with that thing. I didn't unload it or anything."

"Oh man! I'm sorry." He reached around carefully to hold it in one hand.

"You sure we can leave him?"

He laughed. "You see any other way out of here?"

So we left and closed the door. Alan turned the gun over in his hands and said, "I wanted to ask you something, but it's a little weird."

When he asks, say yes, Sergei told me.

I ignored the bear. "Shoot."

"I told you about the reunion we had a few months ago."

Uh oh. My skin prickled. If I had hackles they'd be raised. "Yeah?"

"So, like, Captain Collison had said he was gonna come, but he never showed. We only had an email contact, no phone number, and he stopped answering the emails, I guess. We wondered if something happened to him, but it doesn't look like it from the research we can do. I know you and he worked together a lot and I wondered if maybe you have a way to get in touch...I can forward the info to the guys. He meant a lot to us too, and they'd like to know that he's okay."

"Ah." I relaxed. "I haven't heard from Richard in—jeez, years."

"He might answer you, though. You think?"

"Maybe. He must have other closer friends, no?"

Alan shook his head. "Not that anyone else knows of."

"But he was married."

"Yeah, none of us know his wife either. That was after the war."

I'd only met Richard's wife at their wedding and once or twice after. I liked her, and she and Richard seemed to be really in love. For Richard to go to the trouble of having a wedding, he'd have to be. "I really don't know if I can help."

"Could you, uh...I mean, just drop him an email, or call if you have his number? And let me know he's okay?"

"I—I guess I can do that."

Get his number, Sergei said.

"Can I get your email address so I can let you know?" I asked.

"Oh, I don't use email much. Here, let me put my number in your phone."

I hesitated, but at the first waver in his smile, I pulled out my phone, unlocked it, and handed it over. He tucked the gun under his arm again (I made sure the barrel wasn't pointing at me) and opened messaging and typed quickly. A beep came from his pocket as he handed my phone back. "There," he said. "You've got my number."

And you've got mine, I thought, but I just said, "Thanks. I'll look into it."

Score, Sergei said as we walked away.

Shut up, I told him.

CHAPTER 2
A VOICE FROM THE PAST

O f course, Mom had called while I was out. She had an uncanny sense of when I was on a job that allowed her to call and leave a message and then complain that I was screening my calls.

So when I got back to the house, I called her back first thing. "I just got back from a job," I told her. "Pretty exciting, too. I chased a guy across a rooftop."

Her voice had that slightly echoey headset quality and I could hear music in the background, so she was in her office, or shopping at a very quiet mall. "How many rooftops? Did you jump across like in the movies?"

"Technically, I guess, I chased him from the ground. My partner and a colleague of ours were up on the roof."

She made a small noise of satisfaction, either because she'd gotten past my exaggeration or because I'd remained safe. "I'm glad you know how to delegate," she said.

"Anyway, that's why I didn't pick up. What's up?"

"I have some exciting news."

"Mm." This meant that she'd found someone else for me to

25

go on a date with. I braced myself. If only Alan weren't a werewolf, I could've headed her off by telling her about him.

"I was talking to Mrs. Park, who just moved here from Milwaukee, and she told me that she has a son who lives in Chicago and just broke up with his boyfriend. He's a paralegal and he works in, ah," a pause as she consulted her notes, which I could picture easily in whatever version of her tattered paper notebook she was on now. "Aurora. No, he works downtown. He lives in Aurora."

"Okay," I said. "And what does Mrs. Park do?"

She tried to make the pause less noticeable this time. "She works for a non-profit that is trying to save old-growth forests by working with timber companies to plant new trees. She's their director of public relations."

"Interesting. And how did you meet her? Is one of your restaurants thinking of starting an old growth forest special?"

"She joined our Facebook community."

"Where you periodically post that your gay son is looking for a partner? Or do you just ask every new person who joins?"

"If you'd join it, you'd know. Do you want to hear about Aleum Park or not?"

"His name's Aaron?"

"*Aleum*, you know, 'beautiful'?"

Sergei materialized in his bear form to waggle his eyebrows at me, so I rolled my eyes at him and asked my mother, "Is he?"

"Is he what?"

"Beautiful."

"How should I know?"

I turned away from Sergei, who was grinning, and he materialized in front of me again. Damn ghosts. "Because I'm sure you asked Mrs. Park for a picture."

"I'm not going to prejudice you. You can judge for yourself when you meet him."

"And when am I meeting him?"

Sergei couldn't affect most things materially without a great effort, but he could generate electric currents and move air particles, and so a year ago I'd purchased a ghost interface for my tablet that allowed him to interact with it easily. He couldn't lift it off the table, but he called up my calendar. *Tuesday night is free*, he said, *unless you are wanting to go to dinner with Alan then.*

"You can work that out with him. What am I, your secretary? It isn't enough I find these wonderful eligible young men for you? Let me tell you—"

"If I were straight, it would be so much easier to find someone, I know, Mom, don't think I haven't had those same thoughts myself." To Sergei, I said, *I don't want to go out with Alan. I might call him, just to talk about the old days, but...*

"I love you just as you are, Jae. You know that."

"I know." Although that wasn't entirely true, was it? But it was close enough. I knew that many Korean mothers weren't as accepting of their children's alternative lifestyles; I'd briefly joined a community of gay Korean-American men and the dominant topic was parents, comma, intolerance of.

I tell you, Sergei said, *he likes you.*

"So you'll email him? I'm sending you his contact info."

"Sure, Mom, I'll email him."

"Good. How's work going? Staying busy chasing people across rooftops?"

"Pretty busy, yeah. How are all the restaurants?"

We chatted a little longer. Her restaurants (she and my aunt Hwa-Young owned one and co-managed another) were doing well; they were gathering contributions to make improvements to the church; a new bakery had opened down the street and they had the most divine croissants.

I didn't have as much to tell, but I managed, as I always

did, to scrape together enough to get her to end the conversation while still chiding me for being withdrawn about my life. I didn't have the energy to tell her again that the habits ingrained during and just after the war persisted for a long time, and she had already dismissed that as an excuse anyway ("you're not at war now, what do you think will happen if you tell your mother about how you spend your Saturday night?"). And I had to avoid any mention of Wolftown or extras, so when I didn't have a lot of energy to parse my words carefully, it was easier to speak in vague generalities.

I would have to email Aleum soon, because she would have Mrs. Park check and make sure that I did. "Do it now," Sergei urged, aloud now that I was off the phone.

"I will. But I want to call Richard first."

"Ah," he said. "So you have reason to call cute wolf Alan back."

"Sure. Not because I'm worried about a friend of mine."

"Friend you have not talked to in years?"

"That doesn't make us not friends. Anyway, he sends me a Christmas card every year."

"Ah." He nodded his great bear's head. "In Russia, this makes you blood brothers."

"Ha ha." I sat down at my desk and dug through my contacts until I found Richard. There was an email, but if he hadn't been answering those from the guys, he might not answer from me either. Probably would be better just to call him.

I leaned back in my office chair, headset in one ear. The phone rang and rang, long enough that I was about to hang up when he picked up. There was a beat and then he said, in a familiar rough voice, "Jae?"

"Richard, hi."

"This is a surprise."

"Yeah, I know. How you been?"

"Been better. Been worse, I guess."

He didn't ask about me. I got to the point. "I ran into one of the guys from Kosovo today. He said they had a reunion and you didn't show. Didn't even answer their email."

"So you didn't go either?"

"No." Richard knew why I wouldn't go, so he was messing with me for some reason.

"Oh, good, so it isn't just me you've abandoned, it's everyone."

"Fuck you," I said amiably, but the comment stung. "The phone works both ways."

"You bit my head off the last time I called."

"You were being a dick! That doesn't mean you don't call again."

"I said, 'call me when you're ready,' and you never did."

He'd called right when I'd broken up with Czoltan, and he'd been very Richard about it, which meant that he wouldn't acknowledge that my reasons might be good ones, in particular as regarded my mom, and so I'd been snappy with him and I hadn't called him back, and then I got Sergei and I was distracted for a while. If Richard hadn't recently been such a dick, I probably would've called to tell him about Sergei, but... he had, and I hadn't.

I regretted now having let that come between us, so I returned to the present. "You don't have my reason for not going, so why didn't you?"

"They caught me at a bad time."

Sergei raised an eyebrow at that, a reflection of my own feelings. "Okay, well, maybe you could return their email? At least let them know you're okay?"

"It's been weeks. I'm not going to email them now. You tell them, since I guess you're talking to them."

"Fine." I ignored both his snippiness and Sergei's enthusiastic thumbs-up. "How's Desiree?"

"Still living up to her name." That was a joke he'd made at their wedding: "Desiree" means "desired." She'd countered by saying that he was living up to his name, too, but she loved him anyway. "Her mom's having surgery and she's heading down to Florida next week to be with her."

"Ah, sorry to hear that."

"How about you? You replaced Czoltan yet?"

"Jesus." Sergei also sat straight up, eyes wide.

"What? You don't even wanna hear his name anymore? It's been four years."

"I mean, give me a little warning before you lob a grenade at me."

"Sorry, I thought we were making small talk."

"I wouldn't count that as 'small talk.'"

"Big talk, then. You seeing anyone?"

"As a matter of fact, I have a date Tuesday."

"Heh. Is this one of your mom's picks?"

Sergei shook his head, indicating, I suppose, that I should see Alan rather than Aleum. "Yes. No. I mean, I have a couple possibilities. Nothing's definite yet."

"Good luck." That sounded flat, insincere. "How's the gumshoe business? Catching those cheating wives?"

"It was as many husbands as wives, and I don't do that anymore."

"Oh? What's the new line of work?"

"No, I mean—" I spun the chair back and forth. "I don't track down cheating spouses. I just deliver summonses. It's a lot less, uh—"

"Dangerous? Some husband come after you with a gun? Wouldn't have thought you'd need to worry about that."

"No, I was going to say, 'morally ambiguous.' Like half the

time, the person cheating would tell me about how their partner was abusive or neglectful, but I'd still have to go back and tell that asshole that I'd found proof of cheating. Or there wasn't any cheating, but they were sure there was and I'd waste days following their partner to the office, to their book club, to friends' houses, and then I'd get yelled at and told I'd missed something. And even when the asshole is the one cheating, it still doesn't feel good, because usually those times the one hiring you wants to believe they're innocent. No, it's a shitty game all the way around, so I got out of it."

"Huh. You always had some weird ideas."

"Yeah, thanks. Sorry to get back into morality with you."

"We had some good arguments back in the day, huh? No friends like army friends."

"Sure. Okay, look, I'll tell them you're fine. You want to catch up more, you know, you can call sometime."

"Yeah." His tone made it pretty clear that I shouldn't expect that.

When I'd hung up, Sergei asked, "He knows about Czoltan?"

"Yeah. Richard was one of the few people I told. Commanding officer and all that. Plus he knew I was gay, never cared as long as I did my job. The thing with Czoltan wasn't exactly according to regulations, but he had my back on it. Could've cost him is job, but he didn't care." I gestured to the phone. "Sometimes Richard's questionable morality was useful."

Sergei nodded. "You sometimes have too much morality."

"So you've often said, old-timey Russian mass murderer." I grinned at him. "It's gotten me this far."

"As good an argument against it as any."

"Can't you be positive just one time?" I asked.

He spread his great big insubstantial arms. "I am a son of

31

mother Russia. To know my mother is to know that the world is fierce and glorious and ends always in darkness."

"Great," I said, "I'll call Alan, all right?"

The phone call with Richard made me not want to talk to people for a bit, so I took a couple antacids and walked around the apartment watering my plants. The ritual calmed me down, and Sergei knew not to talk to me while I was doing it. It took ten minutes or so because I wanted to look at each one of them and make sure they were in good health. An important part of the calming ritual was focusing my mind on something external.

When I wasn't thinking about Czoltan anymore, I texted Joelle Clark, a former CPD officer who'd gotten her PI license around the same time I had. We'd hit it off well, so I helped her out with any work that involved extras and she helped me out with official PD stuff, which she still had a line into. I wanted to make sure MacArthur had gotten booked, but that was mostly an excuse to check in because we hadn't talked in a while.

It took her only a few minutes to check, and she reported that he had indeed been taken into custody and was awaiting processing. We chatted a little after that; I told her about the quirky teen drama I'd seen the previous week and she told me about the latest Agents of S.H.I.E.L.D. Her wife read all the comics in that universe and had Thoughts about the directions the show was taking. I enjoyed hearing about the stories through her and Joelle's perspective more than I wanted to actually experience them myself. Aliens and superheroes felt like unnecessary complications to my already over-compli-cated life.

That evening, with some prodding from Sergei, I called Alan and asked if he'd want to meet for coffee. He sounded excited and suggested Seoul Food, but I told him he could pick a place nearer to him if he wanted.

"Everything in Wolftown is near," he laughed. "But sure, I'll introduce you to something new. How about Joe Cool on Wall Street?"

"Sure, I know where that is. Never been inside."

"It's great." I could practically hear his tail wagging. "You like capuccinos? They do a great one."

"I'm more a black coffee person but I'm willing to give it a try," I said. "What time is good for you? I only have a few things to do tomorrow and I can move them around."

"Oh, me too. How about like ten?"

"In the morning? Cause I can't drink coffee after about six or I'm up all night."

He laughed. "Yeah, in the morning."

For a moment I was worried that I'd gone too "old man" on him even though I'm only in my thirties, but he followed up with, "I avoid caffeine anytime in the afternoon myself."

"Cool," I said. "See you then." And when I hung up, I turned to Sergei. "Satisfied?"

"I will be when you are," he said, with a broad wink. Here outside Wolftown, he assumed his human form when he became visible, so it appeared that I had a two hundred pound bearded Russian warrior dressed in dirty leather clothes with a necklace of bear claws sitting on my couch. If you looked closer, you would notice that he didn't depress the couch cushions at all, which made me envy the cushions.

"It's just a date," I said. "It's ten in the morning. We're not going to go back to his place for a nooner."

"Not with that attitude," he said, a phrase he'd picked up from one of the movies or TV series he'd watched with me.

· · ·

The next morning was muggy and a light drizzle had started when I set out, so I had on a light raincoat over my collared shirt (one of my nicer, more colorful ones), which proved unnecessary and a bit too warm when the rain stopped the moment I stepped into Wolftown.

Wolftown in the rain doesn't smell like wet fur the way you'd think it might. Oh, that scent is there, but mostly it smells like any other city, the odors of refuse and old brick and concrete getting stronger in the rain. No smells of car or bus exhaust, which is nice, but when they're gone you realize that they often mask the scents of a bunch of people living in a close space.

It was a nice walk over to Wall Street, which ran parallel to Wolftown's northern wall, decorated with murals. Joe Cool, a coffee shop with a drawing of Snoopy on the window, faced a mural that depicted the famous bull sculpture on the New York Wall Street. In the Wolftown version, the bull stood on two feet, smoked a cigar, and walked on a bed of dollar bills and the backs of smaller people.

I admired the mural for a moment before walking into the coffee shop. Alan, in wolf form with his ears perked, waved me over to his small table in the corner. Shirtless, with the same shorts he'd been wearing yesterday, he half-rose to shake my hand and then pointed at the counter. "They've got black coffee, but like I said, the capuccinos are amazing."

It didn't look like they had much for humans here, so the coffee was probably watered down like Pete did it. "I'll try a capuccino," I said, seeing a chance to score points with Alan and also not have to drink weak coffee. At least the cap would likely have milk, and they had a shaker so I could add cinnamon to my taste.

Cup in hand, I sat down across from Alan. I barely had time to study his muzzle before he was talking, with a big grin.

"Thanks so much for checking back in. And for doing the work. I mean, not the work, but—like, checking on Captain Collison, it's kind of like doing private eye work. I didn't mean to ask you to work for free when I asked you."

"It's fine," I said. His nervousness set me at ease; if he was nervous then I had a little more control of the situation. "It was just looking up a friend in my contacts."

"So he's okay?"

"He's fine. He said it was a bad time and he's sorry."

Alan leaned back. "That's a relief. We were worried about him."

I sniffed the cup and then sipped. The cinnamon definitely helped strengthen the weak espresso, so it was almost like a warm horchata with a coffee aftertaste. I liked it, though. I wasn't sure what this coffee shop did that others didn't, but to Alan's expectant look I said, "This is good."

"Yeah." He took a sip of his own. "I don't get 'em often, but I always come here when I want one." He waved to the barista, a short grey wolf with a bunch of hoops through her ears and streaks of different color running across her cheeks and the top of her head. Those would have to be reapplied and the hoops put back in every time she changed to human and back, which indicated to me that she didn't do it very often. Why would she?

"So," I said, "how did you end up in Chicago?"

"Heh. I should've known I'd get questions when I asked a private eye for coffee." His ears stayed up and he kept smiling, though.

I put my hands up. "Just making small talk."

"I know, I know. Oh, it's not that interesting a story. I guess you know how the refugee program worked. We got assigned numbers and then randomly sent to whatever Wolftowns had room."

"And nothing special for the guys who'd helped the American soldiers." It still made me mad.

Alan didn't fold his ears back or anything, just nodded. "I think most people went to Detroit but I got picked for Chicago. I've got friends in L.A. and New York, but not a lot of us went there. Actually, you know what, most of the people I know in L.A. moved there after, they didn't get sent there right away. It's too bad about the L.A. guys being out on the West Coast; only one of them made it to the reunion. But whatever, I like Chicago. It's gross in summer but we've got nice park space and the buildings have good air flow. I went to school for a while and then I tried out for the Wolftown Watch but didn't make it, so I went the warrant officer route and I'm doing pretty well."

"Cool." I took a moment to absorb all that.

"What about you? Are you from here originally?"

Good. He was interested. "I grew up in Seattle, but I went to Northwestern and then decided I liked it out here better. I have friends here and I know the area. It's a big city but it doesn't feel like one, you know?"

That was what everyone in Chicago said, but it occurred to me after I said it that he might not know what that was like. He lived in an enclosed neighborhood apart from the concentration of the city itself, and if (like the barista) he didn't venture out often, his only experience of Chicago might be within the walls of Wolftown.

Fortunately, he didn't focus on that part of it. "Oh, I applied to Northwestern, but I didn't get in. U of Chicago either. I know they have programs to help refugees and everything, but my grades just weren't good enough. Maybe now I could get in. My English is a lot better. But I'm working, and isn't the point of college to train you to work?"

"That, but also to teach you about life, I guess."

Here his whiskers and ears both flagged. "I know about life," he said.

Oops. "Yeah, I guess you do. Sorry about that." I stared down at my cup.

"Hey, it's okay. I'm usually a pretty cheerful guy, you know? It's just sometimes I remember things."

Like that he'd come to the States and done all this on his own, with no parents or siblings, if he were the typical refugee werewolf. Maybe an aunt or a distant relative, but the way he'd said, 'I got picked for Chicago,' made me think that he'd been alone. "I get you. I remember stuff too, but not as bad as yours, I bet."

"Oh, you guys saw some stuff, I know." He shook his head. "I don't want to make this about that, though."

"I bet you got enough of that at the reunion."

That perked him all the way back up. "Nah, not really, I mean, we talked about some stuff, sure, but we mostly wanted to talk about what we'd been doing since then." His muzzle bobbed up and down. "Yeah, except for Gil, but you know Gil. Or maybe you don't."

I shook my head. "I know the type, though." And I told him about Corporal Lansdowne, who started every engagement we'd had with a muttered recitation of everything that had gone wrong on previous missions and then a sign of the cross.

We chatted for a while, with Sergei mostly silent except for occasional pushes to ask Alan on a second date since this one was going so well. Though it did seem to be going well, I resisted until the wolf said, "Well, thanks again for coming to meet me. I shouldn't keep you any longer. I know you had stuff to do today."

"Yeah, it was a pleasure." I stood as he did. "Hey, if you want to get together again sometime..."

"Yeah!" His ears perked and he gave me a wide smile.

"Maybe like...grab dinner sometime?"

The smile froze, then faltered. "Oh, uh, Sergeant Kim, I didn't want to give you the wrong idea. I mean, I'd love to meet up again, but, uh..."

"Oh, hey, no problem." My brain kicked in without me really thinking about what I was saying, just going with whatever words would get me out of there soonest. "No, I mean, it's cool, let's stay in touch and catch up again sometime."

Super smooth, I told myself as I pushed open the door of the cafe too hard and strode quickly down Wall Street. It wasn't until I'd reached Kennelly Plaza that I thought to say to Sergei, *I told you he wasn't into me.*

You think this is painful? he responded. *Once I walk two miles with spear through my thigh.*

I headed through Kennelly toward Seoul Food to commiserate with Pete, who was always telling me how hard it was for her to find a stable girlfriend. As I walked, I imagined telling her about Alan, and imagined what she'd tell me: "Hey, that's the thing we got to deal with. You shouldn't be embarrassed. He should be embarrassed. He knew about you." If he knew about me and Czoltan, which he probably did since he didn't ask why I hadn't come to their reunion, he knew I was gay. "So he should've guessed that you might be hitting on him. Look, if some guy met up with me for coffee and then I said I wasn't into him, you think he'd be embarrassed? No fuckin' way! He'd turn it around on me! So don't you worry about it."

By the time I got to the cafe and stood in the short line, I'd pushed back the worst of the feelings and I could smile when I stepped up to the counter. "Hey Pete," I said. "Turkey club, please."

"Hey, Mister Kim." Pete grinned all the way along her narrow muzzle. "Diet with that?"

"Please."

"Sure. Who you after today?"

I shook my head. "Nobody. Came in for coffee that I thought might be a date but turned out it wasn't." She eyed the people behind me in line, clearly wanting to ask more, so I tapped my head. "I'll tell you later, but you already talked me through it."

"Good for me." She laughed and rang me up. "Dee will have your sandwich out in a minute."

Dee, another kumiho with fur that was more bright sunset than Pete's autumn leaf colors, raised a black paw to me as she assembled someone else's sandwich. I waved back and took a seat at a table, where I got out my phone and tried to organize my coming week without thinking about Alan.

Sergei, as always, helped. *We have saying in Russia: one is not warrior in potato field.*

I scrolled through my emails. There was one from Dick Mercer, an attorney who used me a lot. *What does that mean?*

Means if you want boyfriend, you must go on dates. Cannot sit home watching other people on TV.

Dick had a job for tomorrow, a quick one, and another that he suspected was going to happen next week. I told him I'd take them. *But also I have to go on dates with people who are actually gay.*

You tell me you do not need boyfriend. But you go on date with Alan. You are not farmer standing in field; you are warrior pretending to be farmer.

Sure, I said. *Whatever you say.* The rest of the emails were junk or things I didn't want to respond to, and then there was one from Richard. The subject line was just, "hey."

Before I could open it, Dee came around the counter with

my sandwich, a pickle, and some Korean BBQ flavored chips. "Eat in good health," she said.

"Thanks." I opened the chips first to savor the spicy sweetness.

Sergei shared the savoring and then said, *So you will be calling this Aleum next?*

I guess I have to, don't I? But first I'm gonna eat.

Also... Sergei drew the word out as I started eating.

One of the nice things about talking to Sergei in my head was that I could do it with my mouth full. *What?*

If you were going on date with Alan...

A date, I said. *You're the one who keeps telling me that dates don't have to lead to commitment.*

Still. Is first date with werewolf in...one year?

About that.

So call him. See how he is doing. Maybe he has boyfriend now and you will not need to think about him every time you see cute wolf butt.

I don't— I cut myself short and focused on the BBQ chips, which were great, light on the spice and heavy on the salt and barbecue flavor. *I don't want to call him. After—four years, I can't just pick up the phone and be all like 'hey, how's it going?' and I'm not going back to Wolftown Detroit anytime soon.*

I pushed back the emotional memory of the last time I'd seen Czoltan. Was there a word for something you were sure was the right thing at the time, but doing it was so painful that you never wanted to think about it again? Maybe "army life," or just "adulthood."

Sergei didn't pursue the subject after that. He had a very obdurate manner that he valued as "Russian stubbornness," but he also had a good sense for when not to push too far. I knew the subject wasn't dead by any means, but at least I could finish my sandwich in peace.

Aleum was open to having a get-to-know-you lunch and I had to admit he had a nice rueful chuckle on the phone as we talked about the awkwardness of our moms setting us up. His offices were on Michigan, so we arranged to do lunch at Tony DiFazio's, a casual Italian place that I knew employed extras. Aleum didn't seem to have heard of it, but I assured him the food was top-notch.

(I didn't tell him that it was owned by Radoslav Bekim, who now went by Rudy, and who had selected the Italian-sounding name to better sell the food he loved to cook.)

I got to Tony's early so that I could pick a good table and a seat that let me watch everyone who came into the restaurant. Old habit; I trusted Sergei to be on the lookout for actual threats, but I also wanted to know who was coming in even if they weren't a threat.

Aleum arrived at 12:09, a minute earlier than he'd specified —he must have caught the light when crossing Michigan. It wasn't hard to pick him out: in the thirteen minutes I'd been sitting there only one other non-white person had come into the restaurant, and that was a Japanese woman in the company of two white women. Besides which, Aleum stopped just inside the restaurant and looked around, and when he saw me (the only Korean man in the restaurant) his eyes locked onto mine.

I gestured him over and stood as he got close to the table. We shook; he had a warm grip and a nice smile. And when we sat, he said, "Everything on the menu looks good. Any suggestions for something light?" so that I knew he'd looked up the place but was deferring to my judgment as the one who'd picked it.

I suggested a Caesar salad to start and the lunch-sized

rigatoni. "It's pasta, but a small portion, and the sauce is worth it," I told him.

He nodded, accepting the order, so I gave it to the waitress (who was probably a werewolf in human form). "So," he said, starting off. "You're a private eye."

Here came the first question everyone asked. I held out a small amount of hope that he would be less predictable, but he wasn't. "What can you tell about me?"

"I'm not Sherlock Holmes," I said. "I don't know where you bought your suit or even who made it. I can't tell whether you shaved this morning with a gas light or electric, though I'd guess electric."

"Who even has gas lighting?" He leaned back, maybe a little disappointed.

"It's a Sherlock Holmes reference. Mostly I track down people and that means I have to be good at knowing what kind of person someone is and what that kind of person is likely to do when they're trying to get away."

This, knowing the kind of person he'd revealed himself to be, led inevitably to:

"Okay, if I were trying to get away—I guess you mean from the police? What would I do, do you think?"

I could already tell that this date was probably not going to be successful. Better questions to ask a private eye the first time you meet them are things like, "What do you like about your job?" or "How is your job different from what I probably think it is if I've only seen private eyes in movies?" or even, I know this is asking a lot, but, "What do you like to do when you're not working?"

But hey, you can only have lunch with the person across the table with you. So I looked him up and down. "You're a paralegal, gay, and single, and I don't know much else about you. But I'm gonna say you're pretty up on the law. So if you were trying to hide from police—well, you wouldn't. You'd give yourself up and work on getting yourself out through the legal system." He looked taken aback at that, and a little dissatisfied, so I went on. "But okay, let's say you were framed pretty well and you felt like your life was in danger unless you could find a certain piece of evidence. I know, that's the kind of thing that only happens in movies. But most likely..." I laughed. "Well, at this point you'd probably come find me. We don't know each other well enough for me to be listed as an acquaintance, the police would have to go to your mother to find out about this lunch, and you'd be looking to hire me to help you out."

He fiddled with his tie and took a drink of water, which meant that I'd hit something close to the mark. "Of course I'd never run from the police," he said.

"You say that, but you've never even had to consider the option," I told him. "You'd be surprised what people will do when they're in an unfamiliar situation." And then, because he looked like he was going to argue, I said, "So tell me what you like about being a paralegal? What kind of law do you practice?"

He was working in family law, which was nice, and that led into a discussion of immigrant families and the challenges they face. The lunch remained cordial right up until the subject of Wolftown came up.

We'd been discussing landlords who abused their tenants and he said that it was often difficult to get the landlords to even appear in court for cases that were small in dollar amounts, "but huge to the tenants," Aleum said, "I mean, like three hundred bucks can mean the difference between comfort and starvation sometimes. But getting the landlords to cooperate can be really difficult, and even if the tenants get a judgment in their favor, it's hard to enforce."

"You know," I said, "not to plug for work or anything, but my specialty is tracking down people who don't want to appear in court. It's mostly not criminals on the run from police. That doesn't happen very often, and when it does, the police usually take care of it."

"Oh. I mean, that doesn't happen a whole lot, like maybe once every couple months."

"That's fine. I have other sources of work, but I'd be happy to help out if your office doesn't have someone to tap for that sort of thing."

"I'll check." He devoured the last of his rigatoni with an alacrity that made me think either he was starving or the food was as good as I'd advertised.

"Though I don't imagine many of your landlords go hide in Wolftown."

Aleum set his fork beside his plate. "I should hope not. Why would they?"

"Oh, people go there because they think cops won't go in, or regular PIs are scared to."

"I read about these silver-laced vests. Do you wear those when you go in?" He leaned forward with a kind of fascinated revulsion that told me a little more about what kind of person he was.

"They're illegal in Wolftowns, actually, and no, I just wear my regular clothes. Not even a bulletproof vest most of the time. The guys I chase, sometimes they might take a swing at me, but mostly they don't know I'm after them so they won't shoot. And they're not extras; they're just hiding there because people are scared of extras."

"Are you not?" He followed that thought down to what he thought was its logical conclusion. "Oh, you said you were in the army. I guess you got training to deal with them?"

"Yes," I said, "but no, I don't have to 'deal with them' any differently than I'd have to deal with you."

That offended him. "Hey, I'm fully human. I can't turn into a monster." He peered at me as though wondering now whether I was as human as I appeared.

"They're not monsters," I said. "And if you picked up that knife and attacked me, I'd have to 'deal with you,' right?" I didn't wait for his answer. "That's as much as I'd have to deal with an extra who wanted to attack me."

"I've seen pictures," he said. "They walk around like animals in there."

"That's how they feel comfortable. You know what, if you ever want to walk around there, I'd be glad to take you."

I made him the offer because I was sure he wouldn't accept it, and sure enough, he pushed his chair back from the table. "Uh, no thank you."

After that, it was just splitting the check and shaking hands one last time, perfunctorily and not nearly as warmly. His palm was sweaty, and I wished I could think of some way to put him at ease around extras, but if I could do that, I'd have made millions in the marketing biz.

He was not good enough for you, Sergei said as I left the restaurant.

I know. It was completely different from the date with Alan. Disappointing, but not embarrassing, although Imaginary Pete was right and I should probably examine why I'd been embarrassed. Maybe because Alan had seemed embarrassed.

"Whatever," I said out loud. I had a job for tomorrow and maybe one for next week, and if I didn't have a date for next week, that wasn't anything I wasn't used to. But there was still a part of me—probably everyone—after a failed date, after a string of failed dates, thinking, *is it me?*

So I went back to something I knew I could do well: my job.

I'd called in the MacArthur summons and now logged in to check whether I'd been paid. The firm had hired me on a recommendation and I had been assured that they would pay "promptly." And "promptly," I discovered, did not mean within one day. I filed that away.

Before I even had a chance to log out of my bank app, my phone buzzed with my mom's number. I debated maybe not answering it yet, but—

She will call back until you pick up, Sergei reminded me.

"I know, I know," I said aloud. I thumbed the Accept Call icon.

"How did it go?" Mom asked.

"How did Mrs. Park tell you it went?" I parried.

"She said that Aleum said there wouldn't be another date."

"There you go, then."

She gave that little sharp exhalation that signaled frustration with me. "Why not? What was wrong with him?"

"You assume it was him? What if something's wrong with me?"

"Jae, I don't have time for this. I have a meeting in five minutes. What was wrong with him?"

The weather was nice enough, breezy (in Chicago, that means you don't have to hold your hat on your head every second you're outside) and warm-ish, so I strolled down Michigan toward the canal. "He was bigoted."

"I don't understand. He's Korean, how can he hate Koreans?"

"Not against us. Against extras."

"Oh, that again."

"Yes, that again." Before she could go on her usual thing about how being extra isn't just a racial thing, I said, "I'm sorry. He was a nice guy, very smart, and I appreciate that you put us in touch. But it won't work out." I didn't think that she was intentionally sending me anti-extra bigots in an attempt to make me pull away from that part of my work and life—I didn't *seriously* think that—because about one in three Americans "has an unfavorable opinion" of extras, and one in three of the guys she set me up with did too. It was just math. But it also meant she wasn't screening for that.

She made a "tch" noise. "Even if you have different political views, it doesn't have to affect your life. Remember Min-Sun who I was dating last year? He hated restaurants. Didn't like the mess."

The sun went behind a cloud and I shivered. "I didn't know that."

"Exactly. I never told you because it didn't matter. I went to work and did my job, and then I came home and went on dates with him."

"That sounds sad. Don't you want to be able to talk about work with the most important person in your life?"

"Work is work. Family is family. You have to have balance in your life."

I grinned, back on familiar ground. "So balance looks different for me than it does for you. That's okay, right?"

She let out a long sigh, acknowledging that she didn't have time to recite this particular argument to a stalemate. "I will keep looking. Do you know how hard it is to find Korean mothers in Seattle who have sons in Chicago?"

"Easier when you aren't strict about what constitutes 'Seattle,'" I said. "Al told me his mother lives just north of Portland."

"It's all the Pacific Northwest," Mom said. "Love you, Jae. I'll talk to you soon."

"Love you too," I said, and hung up.

That went much better than last time, Sergei said.

So I wasn't feeling the best when I got back home. I mean, I already figure that most dates aren't going to go anywhere, but having two crater in just over twenty-four hours was a little much. I'm pretty good at compartmentalizing, and besides that I kept telling myself that the lunch with Aleum had been going really well until we got onto the subject of extras.

And anyway, it wasn't going to be a life partner thing with him anyway. At best there'd be a few pleasant evenings and some nice nights and then we'd discover we wanted different things and go our separate ways.

For an hour I sat at the computer and tried to do paperwork, some prep for tomorrow's job, but I kept staring at the same screens over and over. So I challenged Sergei to a game of chess, which usually helped to clear my mind. I always lost these games ("challenging Russian to chess is like challenging American at eating," he said), but I considered them a success if I even got to an endgame. If I didn't concentrate, Sergei would seize on any mistake I made to shatter my attempts to build a formation and rampage over to my side of the board, capturing my king decisively.

Playing was fun because to any outside observer, it would look like I was playing against myself, with a large bear watching. I set up an old-fashioned board I'd gotten from my father and moved both sides as Sergei told me what moves to make.

I had no idea if he spent the time between moves studying the board and figuring out strategy the way I did. Whenever I moved, he gave me his move in a bored voice. Rarely I got to hear him excited, at which point I gave myself a little exclamation point, like chess notation for a surprisingly good move.

Today I had made it to the endgame when my phone rang

again. I checked it and was surprised to see Richard's number. "I'm going to take this," I told Sergei.

"Does not matter. Checkmate comes like the Russian winter for you in five moves."

"Of course." I thumbed Accept Call. "Richard. What's up?"

"Question," he said. "How serious are you about all this 'no cheating' bullshit?"

"What?"

"Your job, your shamus stuff. Is it one hundred percent no cheating cases or would you make an exception for a friend?"

I pinched the bridge of my nose and shut my eyes. "Jesus, Richard. Desiree? Seriously?"

"I've been—it's been a rough year," he said. His voice got a little distant. "A lot of shit caught up to me." I waited, and after a moment he went on. "Shit, Jae, you were there. You know. I started having nightmares about gas. Couldn't go out in the rain anymore, or snow. Anything falling on me, what's the word, triggered? Hate that word. I'd tell myself it wasn't dangerous but my heart was pounding and I'd get dizzy, start to lose my vision."

"Shit," I said. That was right out of the PTSD pamphlet they'd given us when we got back stateside. "Did you go to the VA hospital?"

"Course," he said. "They gave me some bullshit drug and put me on the waiting list for a therapist. It's a 'non-life-threatening' disorder so I expect to get a call sometime in the next two years."

"God dammit."

"Yeah, what'cha gonna do, it's Michigan. Anyway, it kept getting worse. I thought it was the drugs so I stopped takin' 'em pretty fast, but it kept going. Pretty soon I didn't want to wash my hands. Had to use that Purell before I touched anything. Then I didn't want to touch anything at all. I threw everything out of the bedroom, sprayed disinfectant around everywhere. Can't go outside at all. So you can imagine how Desiree took that."

"She...supported you? Tried to get you help?"

"Yeah, all that, but then she started goin' out. And not just to run the errands. She'd say she was going to the store but she'd be gone three hours. Don't take three hours to go to the store. So I tracked her phone. Went to the store on the way back from somewhere else."

I exhaled. "Okay, but...I mean, she's not going to leave you, is she?"

"She's going to visit her mother next week. She says. She's packing an awful lot though."

"So what do you want me to do? If she's gonna leave you..."

He was silent for a long moment. "I don't wanna accuse her of cheating if she ain't. Things are bad enough. What she gotta put up with..."

"Okay."

"But if she's gonna leave...I gotta know. I gotta try to make one last stand. I love her."

That last had a rough, raw element to it that rang true to me. I sighed. "All right. I've got a job to do this week, but I can be there first thing Friday morning."

"Thanks, Jae," he said. "I owe ya one."

"Actually more like five," I said. "Hundred. Even with the friends and family discount."

"Yeah, yeah, plus the plane ticket. It's worth it to keep her."

"That's what I like to hear."

After I hung up, I sat thinking for a moment. I couldn't say no to Richard, but how would it feel coming back to him with confirmation that Desiree was cheating? Not good. The old sour feelings came back to me. Honestly, if not for that "I love her" he'd dropped on me at the end, I might've called him back and recommended a couple guys I knew who'd take the case. But it might be important to him to get the news delivered from a friend.

"Ah, hell," I said, and started to look up plane tickets to Detroit.

Across from me, Sergei growled. "Play your five moves so game may be over."

One hand still on my phone, I reached out and knocked over my king, forfeiting. Sergei hates forfeits; he thinks games should be played out to the end. So he vanished from sight and from my mind, leaving me with a bunch of pieces on the chessboard and, a moment later, a ticket to Detroit.

CHAPTER 3
WOLFTOWN DETROIT

T he last time I was in Detroit Metro Airport, I was a
mess. I'd made a choice and knew that flying to
Chicago (via Seattle) was the best thing for me, but I
couldn't ignore the ramifications of that choice. I'd come from
the last argument that morning to the airport, getting here
three hours early as a consequence, and while airports are
better now than they were when I started getting familiar with
them—and commercial airports are way better than military,
at least if you have to wait around and spend time in them; not
so much in the efficiency of processing—that still meant I had
to sit in a Starbucks for two hours trying to look forward, not
back. And anyone who's sat in their car inching forward past a
hideous wreck on the side of the interstate knows how hard
that is.

That Starbucks was still there, though if my memory
served, the chair where I'd sat for most of those two hours had
been replaced by a small coffee table and two less comfortable
chairs. Maybe the stink of misery had clung to it so hard they
had to get rid of it.

Sergei had never been to Detroit. I flew a lot less since getting him, mostly because my work kept me in Chicago, but also because it's a hassle to fly with a ghost. You have to go through secondary screening while a TSA necromancer checks your binding spell and your license, and that can take up to half an hour depending on how good the near-minimum wage necromancer is.

The Chicago one was pretty good and hadn't inconvenienced Sergei at all during the procedure, so he was in good spirits. *You wish a latte?* he asked as I stopped at the Starbucks. *Double shot perhaps?*

No, I said. *I'll get a coffee on the way to Richard's, though.*

Thinking about coffee and the steps necessary to get it helped me push memories back where they belonged. I got to the rental car place, picked up my car, texted Richard, and got on I-94.

Of course Richard lived on the other side of Detroit from the airport, northeast of the city in Eastpointe. The traffic around Detroit was as bad as I remembered, but Sergei pointed out that it was better than Chicago, which was a fair point. Still, "better than terrible" still left a lot of room in the "annoyingly bad" range, and it took about two hours to get from the airport to Richard's neighborhood, a cluster of middle class homes straining to look upper class, figuratively turning away from the poorer parts of Detroit and toward the affluent Grosse Pointe suburbs.

Richard had told me this was "the nicest house he could afford on a captain's salary," and that tracked. The two-story brick house had been one of the nicest on the street when they'd hosted their wedding reception there, but four years can make a hell of a difference. An ugly scar on the left side between the first and second stories, along with sagging gutters and a cracked front porch step, gave the impression

53

that Richard wasn't doing as well financially as he had been. Or maybe the PTSD had consumed all his time and Desiree wasn't engaged on the house repairs. At least the lawn was mown, though not much else was going on there: no flowers or trees or anything.

My phone buzzed as I started up the walk to the house with a text from Richard. *Let yourself in*, it said. *Leave the ghost outside.*

I stared down at the ring on my finger. I could take it off, but I hated to do that unless I was going to store it in a very safe place. If anyone with the right spells found it, they could keep Sergei and I wouldn't get him back. Or they'd screw up and unbind him, letting him loose to do whatever he wanted. *Why?* I texted back.

Sergei, of course, saw this exchange. *Leave me here on sidewalk*, he said. *I will be good even if someone picks me up.*

Which is exactly what a dead Russian berserker would say when he intended to be very bad. Or good, to be fair, and I'd never been out of contact with Sergei so I didn't know how he'd behave. It wasn't the sort of thing you often got a second chance with, though. If a police necromancer was called to subdue an escaped ghost, you lost the ghost and your license and probably ended up in jail. There weren't a lot of people walking through the neighborhood, but all it took was one curious one to pick up the ring and listen to him tell them how to unbind him.

Richard texted back. *Put him in mailbox. I'll give you key.*

Why? I texted again.

He didn't answer for the longest time, waiting for me to just do what he said. But we weren't in the Army anymore, so I looked up at the dark windows, figuring he was watching out of one of them, and after about two minutes he texted back. *Don't want dead things in house.*

Spiritual germs were a new one on me, but if there's one thing I'd learned from knowing veterans, it was that you went along with their idiosyncrasies as best you could. "Sorry," I said aloud to Sergei as I walked up to the front door and the thick bronze mailbox beside it. It wasn't Fort Knox, but it'd likely do for an hour. Above the mailbox, previously hidden in the shadow of the porch roof, a security camera's steady eye followed me. So that was how Richard had been watching.

Being left in the mailbox was not as appealing to Sergei as being left out where someone else might find him. *Jae, wait! When I am not connected it is very dark and lonely.*

Like a Russian night? I felt bad despite my joke. *It's just a conversation, Sergei. I'll keep it as short as possible.*

He grumbled but didn't answer or object further. I took a breath and reached for the ring I hadn't taken off in more than three years.

Unsurprisingly, it didn't want to budge at first. Thankful that I keep fit and hadn't gained a lot of weight, I twisted, and with a little abrasion on my knuckle, it popped free.

I could still feel Sergei while the ring touched my fingers. He remained silent as I placed the ring at the mail slot. Letting go was hard; I hadn't really been alone since I'd put the ring on, and I'd forgotten what it was like not to have someone watching out for you every step. But this was only Richard's house, and I'd pick up Sergei as soon as I got out. I took a breath and dropped the ring.

Before it hit the bottom of the slot with a dull clank, I felt the isolation, as oppressive as if someone had slipped a blindfold on me. My fingers reached for the mailbox, but even if I'd wanted to, I couldn't open it without the key that I'd have to go inside to get. I opened the front door.

All the shades were drawn and only one light shone in the hallway that led back and away from the living room. Though dark, the room wasn't cluttered and didn't even smell musty. I got a whiff of perfume that I surmised to be Desiree's, but that was the only part of the room that felt alive. The framed photo of Richard and Desiree on the wall had been taken at their wedding, and everything else sat as still and precisely placed as though I were walking through a recreation of someone's historical home, down to another pair of security cameras in opposite corners.

The master bedroom was on the first floor, if I remembered, down the lit hallway, so I walked down silently on the slightly worn carpet. Before I could knock on the bedroom door, my phone buzzed again. I looked up to see another camera pointing toward me.

Don't come in here, Richard texted. *Door's locked. Go into the study. Laptop.*

I stared at the camera, giving it my best "are you serious?" look. Then I turned away from the master bedroom to the study door, which stood ajar.

Inside: a neatly made up desk with a laptop, screensaver floating around the screen. I sat in the cold office chair and ran my fingers over the clean, bare wood of the desk all around the laptop. No dust. Also no papers, no pencils, no accessories, not even any photos like the ones in the living room. It was creepy.

When I swiped the touchpad, the screensaver vanished to show a program called "WiChat," with a video window and a smaller video window inset that showed my face. In the larger window was Richard, gaunt and pale, sitting on the end of his bed. "Hi, Jae," he said through the speaker.

"I'm surprised you don't have a Silkwood shower for your guests to run through." I got as comfortable as I could in the chair.

He chuckled dryly. "I keep them out of the bedroom. The

door has a security seal on it and all the vents have double air filters. Easier than keeping the whole house clean."

"Even over video, it's good to see you again." I said that as one of the things you have to say, even though Richard looked like shit. You'd think getting germophobia would make you healthier, but he looked like he hadn't eaten in months.

"You look good." He leaned in closer. "Thanks for coming all the way up here."

"Thanks for buying the ticket."

"Right, so. Desiree's at work right now, but she usually goes out to her 'appointment' Saturday morning around ten. I turned on Find Family on her phone so I could see where she was going." He reached off camera to some device, and an image popped up on my screen, a section of a map with one block circled. "Here's where she stayed the longest."

I peered at the cross streets and read them off. "Crescent Avenue and...Taukbashçe Street?"

"Good pronunciation."

"Is this place in Wolftown?"

"Yeah," he said. "Is that a problem?"

"Shit, Richard," I said. "You know it's a problem, and you know why."

He grimaced. "What, you're afraid of running into your ex?"

"Yes!"

"Boo fucking hoo. I'm asking you to give me closure on my marriage. Which is still valid, maybe. I got a chance, at least, to save it."

I leaned back in the chair and closed my eyes. "It had to be Detroit," I muttered.

"You're the one that left," Richard said. "Come on, soldier, man up and do your job. You can handle one awkward conversation. If it even happens."

"First of all." I leaned forward. "You're not my CO anymore. Second, shut up about my personal life, which you know fuck-all about."

He kept his eyes fixed on mine. "I'm asking you to do a job," he said, his tone softer. "And I'm paying you, too, but I'm asking you because I don't trust anyone else to do this."

I exhaled. How bad could it be? Wolftown Detroit held something like fifteen, twenty thousand people last time I'd checked. I was going to be in there for maybe a couple hours tops. "All right. Fine. I'll do it."

"Good." He leaned forward and another map appeared on my screen. "You know how to get there, right?" Before I could answer, a picture of an attractive black woman with a wide, bright smile kneeling in a vegetable garden came up beside the map. "This is Desiree. You need me to send this to your phone?"

"Nah." I brought up my phone and took a picture of the screen. She didn't look like a woman who'd cheat on her husband. She looked like a woman who had every happiness she could ask for in the small world of the picture. I knew without asking that Richard had taken the picture, and that she'd smiled that smile for him, and that was why this was the picture he'd given me to find her. I tried to imagine how I would feel if someone who had once smiled at me that way abandoned me. I found it easier to imagine being the aban-doner, so I stopped thinking about it, said good-bye to Richard, and left.

———

Sergei sulked only from the porch to the car; he could never stay quiet for very long. I set the tablet on the seat and told him to find us a hotel, and as he did, I filled him in on the job.

"You do not think she is cheating," he said.

"If Richard hadn't been so earnest about it, I'd think this was part of some plot to get me and Czoltan back together," I said. "He picked up on that right away and bullied me into getting past it. But it feels like he really loves her. I mean, Richard isn't a great actor."

"People can change," Sergei said. "My dearest friend once thrilled to the charge into battle. He grew to hate the battle cry. One day he disappeared from our camp. I never saw him again."

"Very sad," I said absently. "Also, I wonder how long Richard's been dead."

Sergei's tone sharpened and he looked up from the tablet. "What?"

"He wouldn't let me in the room with him. He claimed it was germophobia—that's a real thing that can happen, sure, especially with the bioweapons we saw in Kosovo—but that doesn't explain why he wouldn't let you in. Plus I didn't smell any cleaning products, and a germophobe's house would smell like ammonia for sure. Or bleach." I folded my hands together. "I don't want to believe it, but it makes sense. Poor guy."

"Ahh." Sergei returned to the tablet. "You think he looks for closure."

"That's my guess. He actually said that exact word, too. Desiree's going to see her mom soon and maybe he wants to be sure she doesn't love someone else before she goes, and then... he can go in peace." I hadn't seen Richard in four years, hadn't talked to him in almost that long, and yet I'd always assumed he would be there, part of my world. If I hadn't snapped at him, if I'd been the bigger man and just picked up a phone... well, I had a chance to do one last favor for him and I was going to take it.

"Hrm. Did you ask him if he was dead?"

"No." I snorted. "How do you ask that? I figure if I play along, I'll give him what he wants and he can go."

Sergei nodded thoughtfully. "How long could he have been dead?"

"The last time I saw him in person was four years ago, but I hope not that long. Jesus. I'll ask Desiree when I see her, maybe."

"If she is not cheating."

I nodded. "I sure hope she isn't. That'd make this all so much more difficult."

It wasn't until I was lying in the hotel bed that night that I put my finger on the thing that was bothering me about this job. "Sergei," I said.

"Da?"

"How did Desiree meet this person she's going to see?"

He was sitting by the window in his bear form looking out at the Detroit night, but at that question he turned back towards me. "How does anyone meet another?"

"Maybe it's nothing." I laced my fingers behind my head. "I haven't taken one of these cases in a while. But...those first couple years with you, I was still taking them. You remember how they go, right?"

He waved a great paw. "Like this. Boring. 'I think partner cheats. Go find out.'"

"Yeah, but...they usually have an idea of whom the partner is cheating with. Right? It's always, 'I think it's Chad from work,' or 'Betty the jetski instructor,' or something like that. Richard had to track her phone to an address. And it's in Wolftown! Is she hooking up with a werewolf?"

"Why else would she go to Wolftown?"

"To become a werewolf," I said.

Sergei and I looked at each other. "But if he suspects that," I went on, "then why wouldn't Richard mention it?"

"Perhaps it does not occur to him." Sergei gave a great bearish shrug. "People who do not live in Wolftowns do not think of these things as easily. In Russia, there are people," he held his left paw out, palm up, "and there are berserker-bears." His right paw followed suit on the other side of his body. "One can become the other, but people do not want to think this."

"But Richard was in Kosovo. He saw it."

"He saw it in war." Sergei shrugged. "If he is troubled by war, perhaps he pushes those thoughts away."

"Perhaps." That sounded reasonable. "But if he's a ghost, he'd be inclined to be more paranoid, not less."

"This is true," Sergei admitted reluctantly. "But what can you do?"

"The job," I said. "But I'm going to keep my eyes open."

Walking into Wolftown Detroit, the big difference I noticed right away was the memorial. The great stone statue of an unnamed peasant breaking free of his chains had once stood in Glogovac until it had been destroyed in the Kosovo war. Refugees, allowed to return to Glogovac to gather their possessions, had organized a campaign whereby each of them took a piece of the statue with them as a personal possession (several of the pieces had to be broken further to be transportable). It took them two years to reassemble the statue, which they'd then placed atop a black marble plinth inscribed with all the names of the dead that anyone could remember. If you looked closely, you could see all the cracks, but from a distance the statue appeared intact. Last year, a pamphlet for tourists told me, the statue had undergone further restoration, filling in missing pieces and smoothing over cracks to restore its stability.

I tucked the pamphlet into my pants and looked for the small group of names that I was most familiar with. There around the back of the statue, toward the middle of the right-most column, were Ali, Merita, and Laszlo Osmani: Czoltan's father, mother, and younger brother. I ran my finger over the names and then walked on through the plaza.

DeFrank Plaza had its share of tourist shops and werewolf-themed t-shirts, but fewer than Kennelly, and the plaza as a whole felt quieter, even on a Saturday. No tour groups wandered the cracked pavement, only single tourists and small families. I took the main avenue north from the plaza and passed a couple chain restaurants and then an Albanian restaurant, an independent bookstore with a poster demanding that I acknowledge the Turkish genocide of Albanians, and a small grocery store with a deli counter from which the smells of cooked cabbage and spiced beef wafted.

Down the side streets stretched row houses, well-main-tained and quiet. As I recalled, the first wave of resettled refugees had been slotted into these neighborhoods where there was space. These had been the ones who'd rescued assets, money or jewelry usually, and could pay.

Farther north, there were two neighborhoods where the remainder of the refugees had settled, including Czoltan. When I lived in Detroit, I'd lived in an apartment half a mile from Wolftown. We'd talked about living together, but getting a permit to live in Wolftown as a non-extra was a pain, and I kept putting it off: his place was too small, I didn't know if it would be good for my new business to have a Wolftown address, any reason except the real one.

He knew the real one well enough. I'd told him my family was a huge part of my life and in the next breath told him it wasn't important that he meet them. Czoltan was bright and empathetic enough to put those two facts together.

The block Desiree had headed to at ten that morning lay another quarter mile ahead of me. Richard had texted a confirmation fifteen minutes ago that her phone was there again, so I didn't have any real excuses. I walked up, dreading what I would find, and looked for a nice coffee shop to wait in while Sergei reconnoitered.

I stopped in at a small, clean place called "Coffee on Crescent" and ordered a dark roast without Sergei having to remind me. Seated at a corner table by the counter, from which I could see the whole cafe and the sidewalk outside, I tried to keep my mind on my current assignment, but it was hard to do.

Even during the war, I'd had trouble with that. I hadn't thought about the war in months, but seeing Richard and then coming back to Detroit stirred up memories. I'd done two nine-month tours in Kosovo, and had been all set to sign up for a third when things changed.

We didn't know the depth of what was going on there for the first few months. All we knew was that the Kosovo Liberation Army, which had theoretically been disbanded after the first Kosovo war, had re-formed in the wake of more and more repressive laws passed by the Serbian government that controlled Kosovo. They'd taken credit for two attacks; in response, the Serbian government labeled them a terrorist organization and began rounding up ethnic Albanians (again).

I got there during a summer heat wave, when the air felt so thick you could barely breathe it, when mosquitoes and flies buzzed around in a constant background drone. We joked that foreign meat must be a delicacy, because they seemed to prefer the foreign soldiers to the native Kosovans.

The biggest challenge—at first—was that after the first

Kosovo War, we were not allowed to bomb freely the way we had then. I thought this was a good thing when we arrived: so many civilians had been hurt by the bombings. But my COs, Richard among them, hated that constraint. Without bombs, they said, we had no leverage to make anyone stop anything.

This came into sharp relief for me when the first werewolf refugees arrived in our camps. We'd had theoretical training in handling extras, a whole six hours that boiled down to "They're as scared of you as you are of them," and "they won't hurt you if you treat them with respect." There had been nothing in the training to tell us how to help twenty people and twelve wolves brought into our refugee camp coughing, some of them bleeding.

The Serbs had been using silver powder as a weapon. Silver is deadly to extras, but bullets were costly to cast and often did not fly as true as non-silver bullets. What's more, they could survive a wound if the silver were dug out quickly.

Silver powder, though, once they breathed it in, would ravage their lungs, drowning them in their own blood. It was a horrible death, one I had to watch many times over starting with that first night. Once they'd breathed in enough, we couldn't do anything but make them comfortable. Humans who'd breathed in silver could develop a variation on "black lung disease," but the extras who'd breathed it would die in days, if not hours.

In addition, the Serbs had revived the old World War II practice of weaponizing lycanthropy, in essence making new werewolves who would be immediately vulnerable to their silver powder. Some of the wolves who stumbled into camp that first day had only just been changed. What a terrible fate, I'd thought at the time. Their lives would be ruined going forward; there was no cure for lycanthropy. There were so many jobs they couldn't get, places they couldn't live, people they couldn't date.

In response to the weaponized lycanthropy, the KLA developed a bio-weapon called K-118 that, uh, the U.S. partly funded, which sent the body's metabolism into overdrive enough to kill someone once they engaged in any strenuous physical activity. Like, you know, running into or away from a battle. Thing was, it didn't work on extras. So the KLA sprayed it around where all their people were werewolves and boom, dead Serbian soldiers. That was also pretty terrible.

But the US was the KLA's ally in this war, so I volunteered to help acclimate the Kosovan werewolves at the Red Cross camp. A noble endeavor, I thought, taking care of these poor unfortunate souls. There were a few of us who volunteered: that's where I met Richard, and I was in charge of a small group of men whose reasons for volunteering ranged from having a werewolf friend in high school to wanting to stay out of combat.

Looking back, I'm ashamed of my attitude. It persisted for longer than I care to remember, because not many of the werewolves spoke English well. It wasn't until a month or two later that I met Basim, who spoke excellent English, and who translated for me. He'd gone to school in London and come back to work with his family's law firm.

A werewolf working for a law firm and handling cases for non-extras. I'd never heard of that in the States (there were extra-staffed law firms, but they handled legal problems for extras). His family were mostly werewolves too (his father had married a human). He knew all about extraphobes from his time in London, where he'd had to register with the Metropolitan Police as an extra and a foreign national. Some racist asshole had splashed blood on his door once.

I worked with Basim for the rest of my first tour. He opened my eyes to the stories of all the werewolves in the camp. They were lawyers and doctors and plumbers and carpenters. They were grocers and farmers and ranchers; they were IT administrators and web designers and publishers. They weren't poor pathetic wretches. Being werewolves was part of their lives, not an impediment to their lives.

At the end of my tour I re-upped and was assigned to the main Red Cross camp, the large one in southern Germany that handled most of the refugees. I heard that Basim made it to America, but I didn't reconnect with him. The people from that camp moved through quickly.

In Germany, farther from combat, we adjudicated disputes between the refugees, of which there were many, and helped them with their paperwork. It was in that camp that I met Czoltan.

He was a skinny 30-year-old who'd lost his family in the first Kosovo war, which was when he'd been turned into a werewolf. The Serbs had used silver powder in that war too, he'd told me, only it hadn't been reported much. There had been small groups of werewolves hiding in the woods until the soldiers came with the deadly clouds, and then they were either captured or killed. He'd escaped once and made his way to a U.N. Camp, where he'd been relocated to Germany and two years later come back to Kosovo to try to heal it.

Since then he'd tried to keep his father's print shop going, had lost it, had taught himself web design and worked for a friend's web hosting firm, had dated but never married, had lived in a number of small, dirty apartments, saving money to move to London or New York. And then the second Kosovo war had come along and all his savings had been seized by the Serbs because his father had been suspected of being a KLA member. He had a computer, a cell phone, and the clothes on his back.

And he had the wolf in his blood. "I'm a werewolf," he said when we were first introduced. "I hope that won't be a problem."

"I'm Korean-American," I replied. "I hope that won't be a problem."

We both meant only that we would need to work together; he (like Alan and the others in that group) was a special advisor to the U.S. Army, a refugee liaison because of his fluent English. But in his answering smile, I saw the beginnings of a relationship of a different sort.

A month and a half later, I invited him out of the camp to a bierhaus nearby. We drank together and talked more freely than we could in the camp, and those nights out became a weekly ritual. It was on returning from one of these nights that I put a hand on his lower back and he flashed me that smile again. When I asked if he wanted to stop in a house that rented rooms by the night, his smile grew larger.

My buddies in the Army used that house for hookups, but between me and Czoltan it became something more than just sex. That first time, he told me, "I'm a werewolf, and I'll always be one. I have to know if that's okay." And he shifted to half-wolf, naked, and waited for me to tell him it would be okay.

I wouldn't have thought it possible a year before. But now I knew Czoltan, and whatever he looked like on the outside, I knew I wanted to be close to this man. So I told him it was okay, and to my surprise, it was much more than okay.

It kept being good between us until we left Germany. I hadn't thought much about what would happen back in the States, but Czoltan assumed that things would continue without a hitch. I wanted them to. I just couldn't make it happen.

My coffee went from hot to warm while I stared out the window thinking about the past. Werewolves walked to and fro outside, and when I saw one around my age, I wondered if they'd been through that horror. Sometimes I'd see a dark patch on an ear, or the way one of them carried their tail, and I'd think I recognized them, but the next second I saw that I didn't.

Jae.

I took a sip of the coffee and grimaced. *Did you find her?*

Several rooms in these buildings are shielded against ghosts. Desiree is not in any one that I can see.

Dammit. I sniffed the coffee and got up, leaving it at the table. *All right, I'm on my way.*

Such a sad day, Sergei said. *You may have to do some detective work yourself.*

What do I even keep you around for? His snark was a good anodyne for the miasma of regret I'd been swimming in.

It is a good question, he replied. *You might release me whenever you like.*

Then who would critique my choice of dates?

Everyone?

I snorted and headed for the block that Desiree was allegedly visiting. *Which buildings are the ghost-proof rooms in?*

As Sergei pointed them out, I thought grimly that if Desiree was in a ghost-proof room, that pointed toward cheating. She might not know about Wolftown's ghost wards, or maybe Detroit's weren't as robust as Chicago's. But as far as I knew, there was only one ghost in her life she'd want to keep secrets from.

Two of the buildings were newer six-story apartment buildings, probably mostly for werewolves to judge from the windows (vampires shutter their windows). Around the corner, along Crescent Street, Sergei pointed out a deli; the back room was warded, he said. That might be a front for something illegal, but it seemed less likely that Desiree would be nailing some guy (or gal) in the back room of a deli. Still, stranger things had happened. I filed it away.

Rounding another corner onto a smaller street, I passed a number of shops and restaurants above which Sergei pointed out three more rooms. Probably offices, but you never knew. Many of the shops here bore Albanian or Serbian names and sometimes had signage in those languages too. I could puzzle out a few words from my time over there, but I'd lost a lot of it. My mind was elsewhere anyway, now fully in the present.

I didn't want Desiree to be cheating on Richard, even if technically it wouldn't be cheating now that he was dead. One of the things I'd tried to hammer into my head during my career was not to pre-judge a case, to let it be decided by whatever facts I found. Lately, though, my "cases" had been mostly chasing down people, so I didn't have to find out anything about their behavior other than where they were. This case brought back a lot of memories from my early PI days, not all of them good.

For example, there aren't a lot of things that people sneak off to do without their spouses knowing. If you believe TV, people are forever trying to hide pleasant things like surprise parties, gifts, and sometimes second careers (I never understood that one). In reality, you can pretty quickly tell the difference between someone who's going out to do something their spouse just doesn't want to do with them versus someone who's actively hiding something.

Flip side: if your only source of information is the spouse, then you're already succumbing to bias.

The last street took me back to the coffee shop where my probably lukewarm coffee sat on the table. Opposite the coffee shop, in our city block of interest, Sergei had found no ghost-warded rooms on this side.

So it was apartment buildings, deli, or offices. The apartment buildings would be a pain, because I'd have to find the superintendent, show him my license, ask if he'd seen Desiree, get permission to interview the tenants in the adjacent apartments to the ghost-warded ones...any step along the way could delay me for hours.

The offices would be easier, because they were technically in public spaces; at least, they were set up to accommodate people walking in. I could ask receptionists and other people if they'd seen Desiree. Plus, if she was in an office, it was less likely that she was cheating. Not impossible by any means—if you knew how many people have sex in offices, you probably wouldn't sit on any common-area chairs.

But both of those required me to be ready to show my PI license if people asked why I was looking for her. Even if she were cheating on Richard, that wasn't illegal and it wasn't anyone else's business. I didn't mind when I was asking about people who'd run away from warrants; they had a date in court and were trying to avoid facing justice. But in this case, I wanted to put off showing Desiree's face for as long as I could.

As long as I could turned out to be ten minutes. I went into the deli and asked the thin grey wolf at the register whether he'd seen Desiree. "She'd have been human form, black woman," I said.

"Got a picture?" he asked.

So I showed him her picture. He looked and then shook his head, completely uninterested in why I was asking. I asked if he had a bathroom in the back and he said, "Customers only," so I bought a Coke and he waved me back.

Nothing in the back looked suspicious except a door marked "Employees Only" that was locked, but a quick press of my ear to the door caught no suspicious noises. No noise of any kind, in fact. If anything was going on in there, it wasn't happening now.

I used the bathroom and thanked the clerk on my way out. Absorbed in his phone, he barely acknowledged me.

Next I walked around the block to the office buildings. This quieter street stood a better chance of someone seeing Desiree, so I asked Sergei which offices he'd detected warding on.

He didn't answer right away, which was unusual, but after a few seconds he said, *First one is number 34, second floor, toward the back.*

Where were you?

What, because I do not respond at snap of your fingers, I was engaged in some sneaking activity?

I could theoretically compel him to tell me what he'd been doing, but that was a tiring activity and put a strain on our working relationship. Besides, if he were planning a joke on me, I'd find it out soon enough.

The farthest back of the three offices, a notary public, was closed, the door locked. No sound came from behind the door. Just to be sure, I checked the other office that didn't face the front, a company named "Junco Enterprises" that gave me no idea what they did. They had a reception room and two offices behind the reception desk, both with clear glass windows so I could see everyone inside, which right now was one portly werewolf, as shirtless as any of those walking around outside. Business formal or even business casual was not a big thing in Wolftowns.

The receptionist, a nice brown wolf, asked what he could do for me, and I told him I was looking for my wife. He listened attentively to Desiree's description and shook his head. "She didn't come in here," he told me. "The building has public bathrooms one floor up. Maybe she went there?"

"I'll check," I said. "Thanks."

The next office on Sergei's list, at number 42, had me climbing three flights of stairs to get to an unmarked door. Sergei made himself visible in the deserted staircase. "You're sure this is an office?" I murmured.

"Da. There is desk, phone, room in back I cannot see."

I tried the door. Locked. "I don't have a warrant to break in. Can you listen at the door of the room you can't see?"

"Shielding hurts if I get close," he complained, but he went through the door.

Technically, using a ghost to look or listen inside an office is a grey area of the law. It's not breaking, but it is entering, and a sketchy sort of entering at that. The police use ghosts and the courts have generally supported their use for reconnaissance (since warding is available, unwarded doors are for ghosts as unlocked doors are for us bodied people). I'm not a cop, but this is similar work, so I felt pretty safe about sending Sergei into the office, even if I didn't feel great about the system that allowed me to feel that safe.

He returned a second later. "There are moans and sounds of sex," he told me. "I cannot tell who, but there are male and female sounds."

"Shit. Well—there must be a window to that room, right? Maybe one of the buildings across from the coffee shop looks toward it."

"There is window," he confirmed. "Shades are down. Or else I would be able to see inside."

"Right." I sagged back against the wall. "What now?"

"Go have coffee," Sergei suggested. "Espresso. I wait here and when they come out, I show you who it is."

"And what if she's in one of the other offices? Or one of the apartments?"

"Check office. From coffee shop on corner, you can see

apartments, da? Watch street. She will be obvious if she comes out."

It wasn't a bad plan. Assuming Desiree was here at all, which I only had Richard's word for. So I left Sergei in the hallway and walked down to a cafe from where I could see the entrance of both apartment buildings. I ordered an espresso and sipped it slowly, to Sergei's appreciative noises.

CHAPTER 4

CHAPTER 4
STANDARD PROCEDURE

The patio of the little cafe looked out onto a fairly busy street, even closer to all the passing wolves I'd been watching earlier. Now I wasn't as preoccupied with them, though; I was thinking about Desiree and Richard and the nature of relationships. Did they always grow stale? As of last year I'd been with Sergei longer than I'd been with Czoltan, and even though it wasn't at all the same kind of relationship, that milestone had still depressed me. Ironically, that depression helped me get along with Sergei really well for a week.

Richard and I had been friends for the better part of a decade, albeit that counted the last four years when we hadn't talked at all. Still, when you spend nearly every day and night for two years with someone, the bond you develop persists even if you don't renew it. There was a reason he was the first one I'd told about Czoltan, and that I was the first army buddy he'd introduced Desiree to.

We became friends out of necessity but we bonded through arguments. We both hated the war in different ways. I hated that it happened at all; Richard hated the inefficiency and bureaucracy that allowed it to continue as long as it did. I thought mediation and diplomacy were key, while Richard claimed that his years of experience had taught him that people listened best to force. These made for good arguments over long, hot nights, and because we kept them mostly theoretical—neither of us having the power to put our beliefs to the test—we stayed friends. There was always an incident to support one or the other of our views, so neither of us ever really won.

But the thing I'd never argued with him about was Desiree. She'd done a tour herself, in Kuwait rather than Kosovo, and she and Richard not only agreed on the way to wage war, but on any number of other things, like children (fine for other people), extras (are people and should be treated as such), and Tarantino (brilliant early work, uneven later but at least still trying to do new things). She seemed perfect for him, and he for her. So as I sat with my espresso, I kept hoping against hope that it wouldn't be her in that ghost-proof room in the block where Richard said she was.

A werewolf stopped near me. I didn't pay any attention at first, because hey, I'm human in the middle of Wolftown. You get stared at. Most of the time, though, the curious bystander will get an eyeful and then move on. This one didn't move, like I was a celebrity or something and he was getting up the nerve to ask for an autograph. So finally I looked up at him, just as he said, "Jae?"

Oh, shit.

I mean, I should've expected this, right? Of course in a city of twenty thousand people I'd be here barely an hour before running into my ex. But I could play it cool. I leaned back in my chair and said, "Uh, hi." Then I realized I should let him know I recognized him, so I added, "Czoltan."

"You look good."

"You do too." He might've been lying, but I wasn't. He'd added a few pounds to his frame, but mostly in a good way, bigger around the shoulders than I remembered. Maybe a bit thicker around the waist, though it was hard to tell under the grey and ivory fur. Or maybe my memories of him had slid back to the skinny underfed thirty-year-old in Kosovo.

"You're here on a job?"

I nodded. "Sergei's doing reconnaissance for me."

"Who's Sergei?"

"My partner. He's a dead Russian berserker."

"Oh!" His ears came up. "That explains it."

I frowned. I'd been going along with the whole "let's pretend like we didn't break up in tears four years ago" because it seemed healthy, but this was an odd turn. "Explains what?"

"He came to see me."

That got me to sit bolt upright in my chair. "The fuck he did. When?"

Czoltan took a step back at my vehemence. "Like fifteen minutes ago. This big werebear with a Russian accent rang my doorbell and told me you were sitting at a cafe here and you wanted to talk to me."

Hey! I yelled at Sergei. *How the fuck did you ring a doorbell?*

It is touchpad, he replied. *It takes some concentration.*

And how did you find him?

You are not only detective in this partnership. He sounded unbearably smug.

"Jae?" Czoltan was peering down at me. "You okay?"

"I'm fine," I said. "Sorry. Just asking Sergei what—"

I caught myself, but he read my tone pretty well. His ears went back and he folded his arms. "Oh. You didn't want to talk to me."

"That's not—strictly true."

"All right then, why don't you tell me what is strictly true?"

"I, uh." I finished the espresso and told Sergei, *Next time I'm ordering tea.* "I didn't tell him to contact you."

"Great. So this was a practical joke?" His voice scraped raw.

"No! I don't think so. Look, I didn't ask him to contact you, but it's good to see you."

"Is it?"

"Yes. I missed you."

He exhaled and his tail swung more loosely behind him. "I miss you too."

"So what are you doing these days?"

"Call center. It pays okay."

"Call center? Are you still doing your design work?"

"For myself." He tightened his folded arms and drew in on himself. "And the call center's not bad. I just got promoted to tier 3. In another eight months I qualify to move to support engineer if I pass the test. That's a twenty percent bump in pay. And I don't have to pay rent."

I'd helped him get the refugee settlement that had paid for his house, but this didn't seem like the right time to bring that up. "No, that's cool," I said. "I mean, support engineer, that's great."

"You still snooping on cheating wives for a living?"

"No," I said automatically.

Ha, Sergei put in.

"Not usually," I amended. "I'm doing a favor for a friend."

Czoltan tilted his head. "Which friend? Maric? Boba?"

"I haven't talked to those guys in years," I said.

Wolves could get pretty smug looks on their muzzles, and Czoltan's right now was among the best. "I know."

I fell right into that one. "Richard. Captain Collison."

The smug look vanished. "Wait, his wife is sleeping around?"

"That's what I'm trying to find out."

"Right, right." He scratched behind one ear. "I sure hope not."

"Me too. She's really sweet. You never met her, did you?"

His ears went back again. "Just once."

We'd broken up right after that, between Richard introducing us to his then-fiancée and the wedding. "Right," I said. "Well, anyway, they've been together since then, so, you know..." I wanted to ask if he'd been in touch with Richard at all, in case maybe he knew how he'd died, but before I could work my sentence around to that end, he answered.

"Yeah. It's nice to hear about a relationship working out."

I sighed. This was going the direction I'd feared. "It's great to hear you're doing well. Really great."

"Uh huh." He hadn't come out of his in-drawn defensive posture. "I'm doing great. So you don't need to feel guilty. That's what you really wanted to hear, right? No guilt."

"That's not—"

"All right. You've heard it. See you, Jae."

"Hey—"

He was already walking away, in the opposite direction from the apartments I was watching. I jumped up, knocking the chair over behind me, and ran out of the patio.

I caught up with him halfway down the block. Being able to recognize him definitively from behind among a sea of grey and brown pelts and tails over very similar cargo and jean shorts said something about our relationship, but I didn't stop to think what.

He turned when my hand grabbed his arm and he didn't pull away. "What?" he said. "I know I was an idiot to come all the way down here. You don't have to rub it in."

"You weren't an idiot," I said.

His eyes met mine, those eyes I used to love to stare into. Hope flickered in them. "Then something's changed?"

"Well, no—not really—"

His gaze darkened. "Yeah. Okay."

"But—"

I don't know what I was going to say, whether I wanted to keep him there or just make him feel better about going, but at that moment Sergei said, *Jae*, and distracted me with a picture of Desiree and a big naked werewolf—wolf form—in the outer office he'd been able to look into. The wolf, black-furred with white patches on his chest and between his legs, held a pair of shorts in one paw and had his other on her shoulder.

"Put those shorts on," she told him with a smile that said that she wouldn't be asking that if they weren't going out in public.

"Yeah, yeah," the big wolf said. "Why don't you take yours off?" The paw on her shoulder slid down her sport top, cupped her breast, then hooked a claw in the waistband of her spandex shorts and tugged playfully.

God *damn* it.

"But what?"

The wolf's shorts buzzed. He frowned and pulled his phone out. *That's enough, Sergei*, I told him.

"Jae?"

The image vanished from my head and I was staring at an angry werewolf, smaller than the one Desiree had just been fucking. "Sorry."

Czoltan pulled his arm away from me. "You know, don't bother. It's fine. Do your job with your Russian ghost or whatever, and don't worry about me."

He stalked away and this time I didn't follow. What could I say to him?

I walked slowly back to the cafe amid a crowd of fur, lost in thought. Sergei called my name once or twice, but I ignored him until he shouted into my mind. *Jae!*

What? I'd barely asked the question when I got the answer. Desiree and that big wolf—he'd put his shorts on—stood in the street both aiming guns in my direction. "Stop! I have a warrant on you," the wolf yelled.

They weren't just pointing the guns in my direction. They were pointing them right at me.

That, Sergei said.

The first thought that flashed across my mind was, *Goddammit Richard, you set me up, you fucking ghost,* but that wasn't going to solve the immediate problem. "Hey, hey," I said. "Desiree, you know me, let's not do anything rash."

I wasn't sure she could hear me over the murmuring and movement of people scrambling out of the way of us. The sight of a half-naked warrant officer and a human with their guns out didn't send people scrambling for cover the way it would outside a Wolftown. Here silver was illegal and any non-silver metal bullet wound would heal quickly. Like a bee sting if you weren't allergic to bees, and if the bee was the size of a dog. Curiosity over what kind of criminal was getting guns pulled on them outweighed the threat of getting shot.

I was curious too, because as far as I knew I hadn't done anything wrong. Even if Desiree couldn't hear me, though, I had my hands up and out, and her gun wavered.

It was going to be okay. I'd explain myself, and—

I was so focused on Desiree that I made the mistake of taking my attention off the wolf behind her. He growled something I didn't quite hear and then yelled, "He's got silver!" and fired.

My reflexes weren't great, but fortunately neither was his aim. I felt the impact pull on my shirt right around the left side of my chest, but he missed anything that would bleed by a quarter of an inch. Lucky me.

Being a private investigator means that you're often in situations where you have to react before your mind has fully finished processing what's happened. So I was half a block away and running as fast as I could by the time I realized that yelling "He's got silver" accomplished two things: one, it gave Warrant Wolf a pretext to shoot me, and two, it threw an actual sense of panic into the crowd. People jumped away from me as I ran, giving him a clearer shot at me. I was going to have to—

Jae, turn left!

I was just going to. I ducked down the street to my left as two more shots exploded behind me. *Where to now?* Before Sergei could answer, I said, *Find me like a deli or a convenience store.*

How far behind me had they been? I ducked right between two buildings and found myself running down a bare alley with no cover. That was not ideal, but I couldn't run back out into the street.

There is not one in this alley, Sergei said.

Thanks. Left or right? Fortunately, the alley gave onto a small park, nothing with hedges high enough to hide me, but at least more options to run.

Across park, right.

How far behind me are they?

I got halfway across the park before he answered, still running, but trying to make it more casual now. A group of werewolf cubs and a pair of vampires under a thick parasol stared as I ran through, but at least none of them chased me.

They are sniffing in alley.

Dammit. Warrant Wolf probably could smell my sweat as I ran by, or some other peculiarly human scent. The park would help, but maybe not enough on its own. *Find me that deli.*

Yes, yes, turn right, one block, left on Marçic Street.

I trusted him, cutting the street corner and almost barreling into a werewolf carrying a big shopping bag. Ducking around her, I skipped around a couple teens, aware that I might be visible at any moment to Desiree and her wolf, and leapt around to the left as soon as I saw Marçic Street.

They saw you, Sergei told me helpfully.

Great. Where's the deli?

You are almost there. And—now.

I slowed, heart pounding, and there across the street was a shop called Dalmat's Meats. Close enough, I guessed. One glance back showed no sign of Desiree or the wolf yet, but—

Hurry, Sergei nudged.

I ran for the door of the meat place and thank goodness, it was open. I hurried in and breathed in the smell of cured meats all around, good strong smells.

"Morning!" a wolf called from the counter. "I don't often see people running to get my meats. Can I help you find something?"

"Uh." I stared toward the door. "Do you have a restroom?"

His ears flattened out a little. "We have top quality meats made by paw. I follow old recipes like back in the old country."

"I'll buy a pound of sujuk," I said. "You have sujuk?"

His ears came up. "Of course." He pointed to the back of the store.

"Please." I made a show of grabbing my crotch.

The wolf sighed. I hurried back to the bin, where half-pound links of sausage lay stacked upon each other, redolent of pepper and garlic. "Two pounds," he called after me.

"Yes, yes, all right." I brought the sausage to the counter and fished out the cash for it. He took twenty even though it was nine dollars a pound and pointed through the door behind the counter that said, "Employees Only."

"Thank you." I grabbed the sausage and hurried back.

"On your right," he called. "Don't mess it up."

I found the little restroom easily enough and squeezed into it, closing the door behind me. There wasn't a lid on the toilet and there was nowhere else to sit, so I turned what I hoped was the lock on the doorknob and leaned back against the wall.

They have not yet found meat store. Wolf is sniffing every door.

Great. I probably had ten minutes in here. I took out my phone and texted Joelle: *Warrant officer after me wtf do I have a warrant? HELP.* Then I added, *I'm in Detroit.* To Sergei, I said, *Tell me when he gets close.*

Joelle didn't answer. I didn't even get the three dots that indicated she was typing. I couldn't afford to expend all ten of my minutes waiting for her to get back to me. With a little regret, I tore off a piece of the sujuk to eat and left the rest behind. It smelled too strongly for me to be able to bring it on the run from a wolf's nose.

As quietly as I could, I opened the door and locked the knob again, stepped out into the hall, then eased it closed. The knob remained locked from the outside, so that should buy me another few minutes if the clerk told Warrant Wolf I was in the bathroom.

The shop's back door let onto another alley, narrower than the last one I'd tried to use to escape, and also smellier. That would help. Stinking brown water had collected around the dumpster there, so I went out of my way to step in the puddles as I walked down the alley. I hoped they smelled ten times worse to Warrant Wolf than they did to me.

I needed a plan. If there was a warrant out, then there was a good chance another warrant officer would find it and come after me too. So getting out of Wolftown was the first priority. Once I was out I could go to the Detroit PD and straighten this out. They were less likely to shoot me on sight.

Probably.

I wouldn't know until I could see what the warrant was, and I wouldn't know that until Joelle texted me back. Or— wait. I did have another possibility.

They are in meat store, Jae. They talk to wolf at counter.

At least that had taken them longer than I'd expected. *Hopefully they'll get stuck at the bathroom for a while,* I said. *New plan: I'm going to try to get out.*

Of alley?

Of Wolftown. I pulled up Maps and traced my finger along a route of back streets. *Can you help me stay on this path?*

He grumbled. *Keep it on phone so I can look at it.*

I just have to make a call first. I checked the map—out of the alley, across the street to another alley, and then a right turn— and then called up Alan's number.

"Oh, hi, Sergeant Kim," he said. A little cautious, but still friendly. "Listen, I'm glad you called. I wanted to say I'm sorry about the other day. I feel like I led you on."

"It's cool. It's fine. Do you have a minute?" The cross street was fairly busy with people walking or on bikes or scooters going about their business. Nobody in more of a hurry than usual. I strolled out and tried to look just as casual. A few were-wolves stared at me, and the nearer ones wrinkled their nose and took some steps to avoid me. Nobody made a move toward me.

"Sure. What can I do for you?"

"Well, uh." I waited until I was in the alley across the way and even then I lowered my voice. "I'm in Detroit Wolftown and I think there's a warrant out for me? I came here to do Richard a favor and now someone's shooting at me. I tried my one friend who can get into the system but she's not answering. Can you at least check and see what's going on?"

"Oh shit," he said. "Yeah, let me see. Hang on, I have to use my phone."

I kept on down the alley and turned right onto a small, quiet residential street, lots of three-story townhouses, and then brought up the map quickly so Sergei and I could refresh our memory. A moment later, Alan came back. "Hey," he said. "Sorry, I can only see Chicago area warrants and there's nothing there. But I got a buddy in Detroit who does warrants. Two of them actually. You want me to text them?"

"Please," I said. The most logical explanation was that Richard had set me up—somehow—but I was clinging to the hope that maybe it was just a bizarre coincidental mistake, that the wolf Desiree was cheating on him with (or not technically cheating) was sent a warrant for my arrest right as I was following them.

While waiting for Alan to get back to me, I kept going down the residential street. It felt like every single werewolf I passed was staring at me, which was normal for a human in Wolftown, but I was on high alert for anything remotely suspicious. I imagined them checking their phone behind my back after I passed to see if I matched the description or photo on the warrant.

At least the residential areas were less crowded. I got to the end of the street. *Sergei, what now?*

I do not know. You are still using phone for call.

Christ. Can't you see which streets lead to the plaza? Can't you go up?

A pause, and then: *Keep going forward. This street is quiet.*

Thank you. I crossed and walked down another block of townhouses, newer this time. Some had pride flags in their windows; others had trim painted lilac and chartreuse and

other distinctive colors. Paintings hung on living room walls
and sculptures sat near the windows that looked out onto the
street. In the last block, everything had been a little worn
down; here the houses still felt like they had youth and life. A
cat watched me go by with half-lidded eyes.

"Sergeant Kim?"

"I'm here."

"Hey, I texted them both. One of them just texted back and
said he's going to—oh, there's the other one, hang on."

I kept moving forward, on to another street with fewer
pride flags and artsy homes. The stone and brick looked
cleaner here, and the furniture and TVs visible through the
front windows looked more expensive. I approached the next
cross street, a small street, and asked Sergei, *Forward again?*

Let me see map.

In a minute. Alan's going to—

Alan startled me mid-sentence with a loud exclamation.
"Oh *Zot!*"

For an immigrant to be shocked back to their native
language is never a good sign. "What? Talk to me."

"God. This says—" He made a choking noise.

I stopped at the corner. "Says what?"

"Why did you have me look at this? Is this some sick mind
game?"

"Will you tell me what the fuck you're talking about?"

"I can't believe how lucky I was. I could've been number
six. Christ, Sergeant." He was getting choked up, emotional,
and I couldn't tell if it was rage or sadness or a combination.

"What the fuck are you talking about? What does the
warrant say?"

He didn't answer. I yelled again, attracting attention from a
pair of werewolves who shielded their little cub's ears and

hurried past. Still no response, so I took my phone down from my ear to look at the screen. Alan had hung up.

Richard must have done something really fucked up, I said as I brought the map back up.

Da. We knew that.

Okay, let's just—get the hell out of here already.

If Alan, who knew me, had that reaction to what was in the warrant, then it made a little more sense that Warrant Wolf had tried to shoot me. Police were known to get aggressive with criminals they were apprehending—especially certain kinds of criminals—even though they weren't supposed to, even though they got a ton of media attention when something went sideways, even though they supposedly had updated their training to emphasize de-escalation. And warrant officers in Wolftown didn't undergo the same training that police had to, or at least they weren't required to. So I could see where if Richard had made up a particularly nasty warrant and somehow gotten it into the system, warrant officers might think, *eh, better off for society if this guy gets shot resisting arrest.*

Which answered another question I'd had, too: what was even the point of putting out a fake warrant? I'd be brought in to custody, they'd investigate, and it would be dismissed. At most it'd inconvenience me for a day.

But if the warrant was something really horrific...say, a crime against werewolves...then there'd be a decent chance that a werewolf would kill me. Which meant the fake warrant was a serious attempt on my life.

Sergei, why would Richard want to kill me?

Turn left up ahead, he replied. *Why do you think I will know this?*

You're a ghost, he's a ghost. I headed up the street and turned left. It got busier here, and the accumulated weight of the

TIM SUSMAN

stares was starting to eat at my nerves. I was used to hunting, having a single target, not scurrying along unsure of where danger was going to come from. *What was it like when you were unbound?*

He didn't answer right away. *It is hard to remember. Many feelings. Some things felt very important but I know now they were not. But you have felt this also.*

What? When? I asked, still scanning the crowd for hostility. Shit, don't do that, looking for someone coming after you is a great way to look guilty. But if I stopped, I wouldn't be able to see who might be coming after me. I had a new sympathy for the kinds of people I chased. At least I wasn't going to go running up to the roof of a building.

It is how you act on all your dates.

Very funny. Maybe hold the humor until we're out of the city, ok?

I passed a store with t-shirts for tourists: "I Had A Howling Good Time," and "I Got Mooned in Wolftown Detroit." When I stopped to listen, the noise of the plaza filtered through my thoughts. I was close. But how was I going to know if there were threats?

You think this is humor? If I told you joke, you would laugh.

Great. Sergei, can you see if there are any warrant officers in the plaza?

Hmph. How will I know if wolf is warrant officer?

They'll have a gun, for one thing. Where are Desiree and her wolf?

Where do you want me? I can be in plaza or I can look for people chasing you. They are not in plaza. I think. He paused. *No, not in plaza.*

I stopped next to an alley, down which a metal fire escape hung in shadows. God dammit. *Go look for Desiree,* I said. *I'm going to the roof.*

88

Jae. Do not go to roof.

I hurried down to another alley, closer to the plaza. *I want to be able to see everyone on the plaza.*

You always say going to roof is stupid idea.

It's stupid when you're running away from someone. Not when you're reconnoitering.

He didn't say anything, letting me process my own stupidity. I came up to another alley and stepped into it. There was a fire escape down near the wire fence at the other end but I ignored it, instead leaning against the cool brick wall. *All right, fine, but you have to come back and show me the plaza as soon as you tell me where Desiree and Wolf are.*

Of course.

I planned my moves in my head. If I could get to the security checkpoint, I'd be stopped there, but at least there it wouldn't be by furious werewolves who'd want me dead for what Richard claimed I'd done. I didn't have any friends in Detroit PD, and I didn't think my Chicago friends would be able to do much if Alan hadn't been able to see a warrant on the Chicago site. Still, at this point I needed any help I could get, so I called a couple detectives I'd worked with.

Neither answered their phones. I left messages that I hoped conveyed urgency while still being in command of the situation. *Sergei?*

I have not found them yet. They are not in two block area around you.

Okay. Show me the plaza.

I had to admit, Sergei's viewpoint was better than being on the roof. He floated above the plaza and zeroed in on the werewolves walking around in their wolf form. Only one of those had a gun, so we watched him for a couple minutes. He walked around the plaza trying to be casual, but with an intent look that belied the affect.

I tapped my foot. *I could go out and give myself up. They probably won't use guns in the plaza with all the tourists around.*

Probably. Sergei sounded as dubious as I was trying not to be. *Wait—listen.*

He moved in closer as the wolf started talking on his cell phone. Risky, because if ghosts lingered too long, the living could sometimes pick up on their presence. As it turned out, he didn't need to linger all that long.

"I don't see him," the wolf said. He listened to the reply. "He's based in Chicago, so I doubt he knows anyone here. He'll be trying to get out." Another reply. "Yeah, I know, fuck that. Humans get their hands on him, he'll get off on a technicality or something. 'All he did was kill some wolves.'" He nodded at the response, lifting his head to focus on a spot across the plaza. "I'll stay wolf over on this side. Keep your eyes open."

Where was he looking? I asked Sergei.

After a quick search, we spotted the other warrant officer, a tall woman in human form with an equally intent expression. She wore a leather jacket that could easily have concealed a shoulder holster.

I do not think this plaza will be safe, Sergei said.

I leaned back against the wall. *No. Me neither.*

CHAPTER 5
THE VIEW FROM THE ROOF

A ll right. I needed time to regroup. There were people
out there who wanted to kill me rather than let the
police apprehend me for a horrible crime I hadn't
committed. Two were blocking the only way out of Wolftown
and one—two—were actively hunting me.

This did not seem like a good situation.

I'd had the thought many times that a Wolftown was a
terrible place for anyone being chased to go. There was only
one entrance and it was guarded by security personnel. Probably for exactly that reason police chases never ended in
Wolftowns, even when the person being chased was an extra.

There were rumors, though, of places where you could go
in and out without passing the security barriers. Several of
these had been found in the sixties, old sewer lines and an
abandoned spur of a subway line that some enterprising werewolf had dug down to. The news of them being found always
ended the same way: "The Wolftown Civic Authority sealed up
the unauthorized access." In the last twenty years, as far as I

was aware—and I kept up on Wolftown news—no more had been found.

People still talked about them, though. Sometimes I heard whispers that the tunnels hadn't been sealed up as solidly as the news would have you believe, that the WCA had made a show of it for public relations while quietly leaving an emergency exit for the extras who might need it.

In a place like Chicago, where the WCA worked paw in hand with the city council on pretty much everything, there was zero chance that someone like me would ever find out about those emergency exits if they even existed. But in Detroit, where every stage of the refugee resettlement program included at least one politician who'd tell us how much the city and Wolftown had a "tense" or "strained" or even "hostile" working relationship? Seemed like a better than zero chance, and that was enough to send me to my phone searching for that article about the "Secret Passages of Wolftown."

Sergei, I said as I skimmed, *any update on Desiree and Wolf?*

I have not seen them.

Are you looking? The article was vague, probably intentionally, about where these passages were. The Detroit one was a sewer that had come out in "the basement of an apartment building." What apartment buildings had been around in the sixties? Were they still around?

I am now.

Thank you. I wished I could think of someone familiar with the history of Detroit Wolftown, but everyone I knew who lived here had been here less than a decade. The Internet wasn't much help; "history of Detroit Wolftown apartment buildings" didn't give any useful results, nor did "Detroit Wolftown apartment buildings with basement."

Think think think. I stared at my phone and the search

engine, looking up every time someone walked by the mouth of the alley, which was frequently enough to make me feel very jumpy.

Storyteller in Russian village knows all history, Sergei said.

Great, I said, and started to type in "Detroit Wolftown storyteller" just to show him that that wasn't going to bring up any results, it being more than a hundred years since his story-teller had died, but then in the middle of my spiteful typing I thought, wait. We do have storytellers. They're in museums.

I changed my search to Detroit Wolftown Museum, and thank the god of idiots in trouble, there it was. It wasn't too far, but it was on the opposite side of the plaza from where I was.

At least it was a tangible goal that I could make my way to, which was preferable to standing here waiting for Joelle to text me back. I checked in case I'd missed a notification, but she still hadn't responded. I added another message telling her that it was urgent and could she please please look into it, and then pocketed the phone.

They are one block away, Sergei informed me.

One block? I stared down the alley toward the street, then in the other direction. This was not one of those alleys that connected two streets; perhaps it once had, but now a large wire fence separated this half of the alley from what looked like a collection of dumpsters. I could climb the fence given time, but could I do it before an angry werewolf came around the corner with a gun and an itchy trigger claw? I didn't think so. *Thanks for the warning. Do I have time to get out into the street?*

They are moving slowly, Sergei said, *and I am not used to being prey. We are always hunting, not running.*

I didn't choose this. I eyed the fire escape. *I don't want to climb to the roof.*

No. Go to the street now and get across quickly into a store. They have back doors that exit into small street. Stores on this side do not. I will tell you if they see you.

People still walked by the mouth of the alley. I straightened my shirt and walked out into the wide street, trying to look as natural as a human walking out of an alley in Wolftown could. I got plenty of looks but tried to ignore them, saying, "Excuse me," as I made my way across the street with the (I hoped) appropriate mix of haste and nonchalance, as if I had a goal in mind that wasn't just "away from the people chasing me."

Someone grabbed my shoulder. I wrenched away and turned, already breathing faster, to see a short middle-aged werewolf with their ears back and nose wrinkled, looking puzzled. "Whoa, buddy," they said in a light voice. "Nobody's gonna hurt you here."

"I know." They looked to be in about their early twenties, with a Banana Republic t-shirt and shorts on and a wide-eyed perked-ear helpful expression. "I'm just, ah, I'm in a hurry."

"I thought you might be lost. The plaza's back there, if you're looking for your tour group."

I looked over their shoulder and couldn't see Desiree anywhere, nor anyone who seemed to be hunting. "No, I'm here on business, actually. I'm, ah, looking for someone and I need to—"

They are close, Jae.

"I gotta go," I concluded, and speed-walked from the bewildered werewolf to the opposite side of the street.

Five storefronts faced me: two boutique clothing stores, a bookstore, an antique shop, and a beautician. No alley between them, nowhere anonymous to duck into.

Hurry, Sergei snapped, and without looking back I ran for the bookstore.

The small shop had no air conditioning (not running, at least), only a fan blowing over an Airwick or something that filled the room with a pleasant grassy smell. I hoped it would cover my scent at least a bit, but as I lingered back in the Non-Fiction section, from where I could see the door through two bookshelves, I noticed the distinct aroma of garbage.

At first I thought there was a trash can nearby, but a moment of sniffing traced the smell to my shoes. That was why that wolf in the street had their nose wrinkled: a human wandering around smelling of garbage. They probably thought I'd wandered into Wolftown somehow to panhandle or just to sleep in one of the relatively uncrowded alleys for the night. The Paranormal Guard weren't always picky about who they let in.

Feeling slightly guilty, I kicked off the shoes and walked over to Mysteries in my socks. The smell didn't follow me as far as I could tell, but then again my nose was about a hundredth as sensitive as a wolf's. Still, it was the best I could do for the moment.

They are following you into the store.

Their shapes loomed in the bright day outside and then the two of them entered the store. They went to the clerk at the counter, where Warrant Wolf showed her his authorization and she pointed vaguely to the back of the store.

Seeing Desiree again brought on the urge to explain myself, to ask her to consider that the charges weren't necessarily true. If I could get her away from the wolf for a few seconds, I didn't think she'd shoot me, and maybe I could explain myself so she'd protect me when the wolf came back with his itchy trigger paw-finger.

The wolf went right for the Non-Fiction section, where he found my shoes. Desiree lagged behind, and in the small store —especially with the clerk now watching for me as well, with wide scared eyes and flat-back ears—I had to take a split-second opportunity where I could find it.

It's hard to know how fast of a run will be threatening to someone when ideally you'd like to walk toward them calmly with your hands out, but you know you don't have enough time. I like to think it's one of those problems without an actual solution, because I sure as hell didn't get it right.

I'd crossed half the store toward Desiree when she turned and saw me. Her reaction wasn't what I'd hoped for; she sprang back into one of the bookshelves, making a clatter and knocking a few books to the floor.

"Listen," I said hastily. "Just hear me out, okay? I didn't do it, whatever it is. I swear to you."

"Get away from me," she said, and her voice *shook*. She gripped the shelf behind her and half-turned to the side without taking her eyes off me. Sweat glistened on her brow. "Galen!"

"I'm innocent!" But I was already backing toward the front door as Warrant Wolf—Galen, I suppose—came around the shelf, his gun raised.

The clerk behind the counter made a kind of whimper-squeak that in retrospect might have saved my life. Galen kept his gun on me but his ears came up at the noise. "We shouldn't make a mess in here," he said, with an eye on me, "but I will if you don't do exactly as I say. You got a back door?"

This was to the clerk. She nodded and pointed behind him, toward the back of the store.

Do you think I can make it through the front door? I asked Sergei, sensing the warmth of the sun through the glass doors on my back. My lizard brain yelled at me to run and it was proving difficult to ignore it on my own.

Can you run faster than bullet?

Galen gestured with his gun, the way people who haven't handled guns a lot think they should because they see it in movies. "Get to the back," he told me.

96

There weren't any convenient shelves to duck behind, just small tables piled with books. I could maybe jump behind one of those and avoid his first shot, but eventually I'd have to run to the door and he'd have a clear line of fire. My only chance was my partner. *He's going to shoot me in the alley.*

Get ready to run, Sergei said, deadly serious.

He knew what I was asking; we'd used this trick before, though never in as serious a situation as this. *Go*, I told him.

"Move!" Galen yelled at me, and at that moment a seven-foot tall Russian bear materialized between us. Sergei roared and charged as I ducked to my right. Galen fired twice; the bookstore clerk shrieked and I presume that she dove behind her counter, but I wasn't watching as I ran for the front door. The two shots had left the window next to the front door riddled with spiderweb cracks, but the door itself was undamaged. I yanked it open and ran out.

On the street I wove between startled werewolves and a pair of kishi (maybe bouda; even with time to look more closely, were-hyenas look pretty similar). I didn't have a plan, but the street was rough on my feet in just my socks, so I made a decision and took a sharp right into the antique store.

The clerk, an older coyote, half-stood from his chair as I ran in. 'Sorry," I panted, "it's an emergency." I ran toward the back, hoping Sergei was right about these shops having a back door, hoping that Galen and Desiree didn't think to intercept me around back.

"The restroom's locked," the coyote said, but I'd already spotted a dusty back door and seconds later had my hand on it.

They have gone out front, Sergei told me.

I eased open the back door and slipped through it, ignoring the calls from the coyote that died out as I closed the door. Here was another alley, cleaner, the concrete cool below my socks. Dumpster receptacles dotted the pavement and, most importantly, not a single other person was visible down either end.

If I remembered my map right, I wanted to head across the alley and keep the plaza on my right as I tried to evade pursuit. I wasn't at all sure that the museum was going to help me, but it had two advantages: one, I was pretty sure they wouldn't expect me to go there, and two, it was a tangible goal to keep moving toward.

Wolf is going into stores. Not antique yet but only one away.

Shit. Galen wasn't half bad at pursuing a suspect. It was a wide street and I hadn't had much of a head start. When he didn't see me right away, he'd guessed that I'd ducked into one of the stores, and I'd bet he left Desiree outside to watch in case I came out while he was inside.

The problem with getting across the alley was that although the stores on this side had back doors that opened onto it, probably they were locked from the outside. And the buildings across the alley looked to be apartments; none of them would let me in. So I'd have to go down the alley until I found a cross street or a space between buildings.

With no time to waste, I strode quickly away from the plaza, heart pounding from fear more than exertion, armpits and lower back sweaty. I'd had guns pointed at me before, but almost never—since Kosovo—by someone who'd stated their intention to shoot. You'd think that military experience would lessen the impact, and it did help me act under pressure by freezing the parts of my brain that were scared so I could, for example, run for the door while Galen was shooting at Sergei.

The thing is, those parts don't stay frozen forever. While I expected people to shoot at me in Kosovo, I was a lot less used to it happening in a civilian environment, much less a pedestrian street or the quiet of a bookstore. So that was threatening to freak me out, while the military-trained part of me was trying to keep the panic frozen with promises that we'd be out of this soon and then when we were safe, we could panic.

"Soon," though, kept being pushed farther and farther out. I could keep myself in control for a while longer, but I knew from my own experience and the experiences of many others that eventually that panic would unfreeze. You couldn't stay in a state of high alert and fear forever without any consequences.

If I could get away from them and get to the museum, have a place to hide and form a plan, that would help more than the time in the alley had done. But first I had to—

Wolf is in antique store. Coyote is pointing to back door.

Shit. I abandoned any pretense of not being a fugitive and fled for the end of the alley.

Keep going, Sergei urged.

Too harried to respond sarcastically, I rounded the corner at a run. A werewolf in a vest and shorts jumped out of my way; I apologized and hurried on. "Chill, dude," the wolf said.

More wolves and a few other extras walked up and down this street and though I tried to hide among them, I had no illusion that I wouldn't stand out to the most casual of glances. *Did he see me?* I asked Sergei as I scanned for more places to hide along the street.

Yes.

I didn't say, "Thanks for telling me so quickly," but Sergei understood. *He paused to talk on phone*, he told me. *But now he runs to street you are on.*

Ahead of me, a large intersection bustled with people. The shortest way to the museum was across it; as a bonus, the mass of people might mask my scent. Without my garbage shoes, maybe I'd be harder to track (though I stank of my own sweat now), and as long as I stayed a little hunched over, I'd be shorter than most of the wolves on the street. Without a ghost to watch from above, I hoped Galen would lose me quickly.

As I crossed the intersection, I glanced to either side out of habit. What I saw to my right, in the direction of the entrance, distracted me enough that I stumbled on the street and almost fell into a wolf couple. A wolf—not Galen—was running down the street toward me. Still fifty feet away, but closing fast.

There were any number of reasons someone might be running down a street, but I thought this was the wolf Sergei had shown me in the plaza. Even if it wasn't, they were running with a purpose, and Galen had just been on the phone, maybe calling in help with the chase.

I stubbed a toe when I stumbled, but I ignored the pain and sprinted through the intersection, dodging people as I went. *After pink awning*, Sergei said, *there is gap to left*. He paused. *And place where you can get to roof.*

I'm not—oh, fuck it. At least two of them were too close, and who knew if someone was coming toward me on this very street. The sooner I got out of here, the better. Maybe the roof would be a temporary respite and I'd get to the museum, or maybe I could stay there long enough to catch my breath. Maybe Joelle would text me back. *Are there connected rooftops?*

Yes.

I saw the pink awning and ran around it. There, on the side of the three-story building, two crates sat below what looked like a flimsy metal ladder attached to the brick. I hesitated. *Do I have time?*

If you stop asking questions.

So I jumped up on the crates, ignoring the sharp prick of a splinter in the ball of my foot, and grabbed the first metal rung. There's no way this ends well, I thought.

I clambered up the ladder, for the first time feeling a little fatigue even with the adrenaline coursing through me. My arms, relatively fresh, made up for the lack of energy in my legs, pulling me up to the edge of the roof. I clambered over and onto the warm tar-paper and lay there for a moment. *How much time do I have?* I asked Sergei.

Galen is still sniffing, he replied.

I got to my feet and resisted the temptation to look down over the edge (that was something that people I chased who went to the roof often did, giving themselves away), instead walking over to an HVAC exhaust to orient myself. The plaza was over there, so the museum would be...there.

That side of the roof, fortunately, abutted another building of the same height. I jumped across to the other roof and kept going, at a slower pace now that there was less urgency. I wasn't going to be able to make it all the way to the museum across rooftops but I could get at least to the end of this block.

With the sun out and my recent exertion, I was much more aware of my sweating. I loosened my shirt to let the breeze in and took deep breaths of air. Leaving behind the rooftop I'd climbed onto gave me a sense of having ditched my pursuit, which intellectually I knew was false, but which was too welcome a relief to deny. Maybe there was something to this roof thing.

Barring a cluster of taller apartment buildings, I could see across all of Wolftown from up here, tracing the line of the concrete wall from the entrance plaza around to the river on the other side and back to the entrance, an unbroken line. No way through except the entrance, but maybe a way under if I were lucky.

And inside this defined space resided almost twenty thousand extras, along with a bunch of tourists, Desiree, and myself. I crossed one more roof before I came to an intersection that I couldn't jump across.

According to the map on my phone, the museum was not

too far; four blocks up and two over once I got down to the ground. There was another fire escape on this building, not too far from me, but I didn't want to go down until I was sure Galen wasn't going to be waiting. So I asked Sergei to sniff around for me and I took a seat on the edge of the roof (facing in, not out), enjoying the stiff breeze and the respite.

Joelle still hadn't texted me back. I stared at the three messages I'd already sent her and opted not to send a fourth. When she turned her phone back on she'd text me (unless, my brain whispered, she believes the charges...). Until then there wasn't anything I could do except carry out my own plan.

I scrolled through the contacts on my phone, thinking there had to be someone else I could text, but nobody came to mind. A full two thirds of the contacts were people I hadn't talked to in years: old college friends, old Army buddies, ex-boyfriends. The rest were professional contacts—while having a half-dozen lawyers would be useful if I were taken into custody, they wouldn't be able to do much to make sure I got that far— and family. Mom was the worst person I could call from here; she'd be unable to help, would make me feel like somehow this predicament was my own fault, and would take it as final proof that Wolftowns Are Dangerous forever and ever amen.

The thought had often crossed my mind that having Sergei around made it very convenient to stay in without getting lonely, to act like a reclusive married couple without actually having a marriage. The job of a private investigator—the private nature, the odd hours—also made it harder to make friends.

Do not blame me, the Russian ghost said. *I tell you to go meet people.*

How's it looking?

The situation was serious enough that Sergei didn't even

deliberately misconstrue my meaning. *He is talking to people in the street. I think perhaps he has lost your scent.*

Fantastic. Maybe roofs were only a bad idea if you were being chased by someone smart enough to—

He is near the alley.

I sat up straight and held my breath. Even though I was sitting on the edge, I was pretty sure that I wasn't visible from the street, never mind from the alley three houses over. But still, close to the alley was close to the ladder I'd climbed up, and if he could track me there, he could find me. The three rooftops I had all to myself now felt like a prison just like Wolftown itself, smaller and less escapable.

The nearby fire escape on my building beckoned. I didn't want to tell Sergei to leave Galen even for a moment, but I also didn't want to expose myself if there was someone below looking up. The chances of that were vanishingly small, though, weren't they? So I crept over to the curved metal railings, gripped them, and cautiously peered over.

Nothing. The alley below was empty.

Sergei, I'm going down.

Da, he said. *Was just about to suggest this.*

Where's Galen?

In alley. He is sniffing and now is talking on phone.

What's he saying?

A mental sigh from the bear. *I will move closer—no, he has put phone away now. Now he is moving to fire escape. First one you used.*

Gotcha, I'll go.

I swung myself over the edge, trying to minimize the clang; my socks didn't make any noise, but the whole fire escape rattled with my weight on it. Probably it hadn't been maintained in twenty years or more. That thought made me keep my feet to the edges of the rungs for maximum stability as I descended.

At the first balcony I stopped and looked over the side. Nobody below me still. Good. No, wait—a human had stopped at the entrance to the alley and now looked in. Casually at first, but then their eyes traveled up and spotted me and they stopped dead, their entire being focused on me.

With a chill, I recognized the woman in the leather jacket who'd been talking to the other warrant officer in the plaza. My hands and feet started climbing again even as my brain was trying to figure out whether I'd be better off on the roof or trying to get past her in the alley.

One of the other officers is over here in this alley, I told Sergei, clambering over the edge of the roof. *She saw me.*

Vot blin, Sergei swore, an expression that I think literally translated to "here pancake" (according to Google) but actually meant, "shit." *Galen is climbing ladder as well. I will...look around.*

There aren't any other fire escapes, I said, standing on the roof and staring desperately around. *And I don't think the Russian bear trick will work again.*

Not if there are two on opposite sides.

There wasn't even anything for me to hide behind. A couple HVAC exhaust assemblies, each about two feet high. I could squat down behind one, but that wouldn't help past the five seconds it would take one of the officers to walk toward it.

Behind me, the fire escape rattled as the woman got onto it. The noise stopped, but I knew she was climbing up, and Galen too. I had maybe fifteen seconds.

"Jae."

Sergei's physical voice came from behind me. I turned.

He stood at the edge of the roof at the back of the middle building and beckoned. I ran toward him and as I did he pointed behind him, off the edge, and then vanished. *There is a pile of trash there. Bags contain much cardboard and styrofoam, nothing very hard. You would have to jump twelve feet.*

I can do that. I wasn't at all sure that I could, but the alternative was—

"Stop right there!"

Galen pulled himself up over the roof of the next building over, the one I'd originally climbed up on. I noted that he had the good sense not to try climbing with his gun in one paw; he stood on the edge of the roof and pulled it from its holster, pointing it at me.

The place Sergei had stood was ten or fifteen feet away, about the running start I'd need. I didn't want to make that jump, though, so I tried one last time. "I'm innocent!" I yelled.

"Sure you are." Galen kept his gun level, his ears perked forward at me. "They all are. We'll just get you to the cops and they'll decide."

"Right, so that gun's just for show?" I kept an eye on the woman, who also had her gun out.

"You're armed. You want to drop your gun, we'll drop ours."

"What makes you think I even have a gun?"

"Says so in the warrant."

"Which is completely fake." I edged toward the place where Sergei had stood. "Don't suppose you'd care to tell me what's in it."

"I said stop moving!"

"Why? Where are you afraid I'll go?" Both of them stayed right next to their fire escapes, and had no doubt checked that there weren't any other exits from the roof.

"He's got a point," the woman said. "If he jumps, it saves us a bull—" She swallowed the end of "bullet," with a look at me. "A trip to the station."

"You'd still have to take my body," I pointed out. "It'd be harder, if anything."

I was pretty sure that the only thing stopping Galen from shooting up to that point was that he wasn't sure he could hit me. At that comment, though, he stopped and his ears flicked back. Clearly he hadn't thought about how he'd get a dead body down from the roof. After a moment, his ears came back up and he lowered his gun. "Come over here," he said. "We'll all climb down together and then we'll go to the police."

Directly behind me? I asked Sergei.

Da.

"You know, that's an awfully tempting offer," I said. "But I don't really want to die in an alley."

I turned and sprinted for the edge of the roof. Galen said something in reply but I didn't hear it with the wind in my ears.

I did hear two gunshots from his side and one from the other. All three missed, though I fancied I could feel the hissing of the bullets as they went by me. I made it to the edge of the roof and jumped.

I'd been counting on being able to see the pile of garbage Sergei'd told me about when I got to the roof so I could make minute adjustments to land there. What he hadn't told me was that the pile of trash was over the fifteen-foot chain-link fence a couple feet behind the buildings.

So as I got to the edge of the roof, bullets whizzing by me, the minute adjustment I made was to lean forward and propel myself farther out. I had to clear that fence or else I'd land on concrete and Galen would either have the corpse he wanted or a very good cover to kill me. Or I'd impale myself on one of the loose ends of the chicken wire and end up draped over the fence and bleeding. That'd make it hard for Galen to get me down, anyway.

All of these thoughts went through my head between the moment I pushed off from the roof and the moment I watched the fence slide under me in what felt like slow motion. Then I got to shift my attention to the piles of garbage bags rising up to meet me, stacked high like a mountain over the sides of a large bin.

The complete extent of me thinking about people jumping onto garbage bags was a handful of "you don't know what's in that bag" during various movies and TV shows over the years plus one really bad afternoon with some friends at the age of 13 that ended with all of us going home to take showers. Now, as I cleared the fence, my worry was split between "what's in those bags really?" and "am I even going to hit them?"

The second question, more pressing, was answered mostly in the affirmative. I managed to twist my body to land on my back, protecting my head, and landed not quite dead center on the pile of garbage bags, hard edges and corners with give. Cardboard and styrofoam, as Sergei had promised. Momentum carried me a little way and then bags slid out from under me and my left leg smacked hard into the side of the bin. Fortunately, the pile had already partly broken my fall, so I was left with only a bruise and (probably) not a fractured tibia.

I lay on the trash, winded by the fall and somewhat stunned that a bruised shin was the worst injury I'd gotten from it. Then my arm and hip flared with stabs of pain and I found a box poking into my hip and a torn sleeve with scraped skin below it. I couldn't tell what had caused the scrape, which worried me in a trash bin, but possibly infected with some gross bacteria was better than dead on a rooftop.

A gunshot rang out as I thought that, making the chicken

wire fence clang and shudder. A glance at the roof showed two silhouettes there.

Dead in a garbage bin was no better than dead on a roof. I scrambled out and my bruised shin objected, sending me to one knee, which was fine because then the bin shielded me from the roof. I didn't think either of them would jump down —hell, if they hadn't been shooting at me, I wouldn't have— but once I got going they would for sure be on my tail again.

Nobody else had seen me fall that I could tell; the bin sat in a small area that looked to be shared by several small restaurants. A very narrow alley led along the chicken wire, but I didn't want Galen and his friend to be able to see where I was going, so I picked one of the back doors at random and ran for it.

Thankfully it opened, letting onto a hallway that smelled of fried chicken and reminded me that I hadn't eaten in a while. No time for that now, as tempting as it was to grab something off one of the plates stacked by the sink in the kitchen. A wolf shoving them into a steam dishwasher looked up and gave a startled, "Hey," as I went by.

"Sorry," I said, and navigated my way into the main body of the restaurant, hoping I looked like a customer who'd gotten lost.

Not really; this restaurant was a counter-service place that —despite being close to the plaza—was filled with extras. Mostly wolves, a quartet of vampires, a pair of kushtaka. One customer appeared at first glance to be a deeply tanned human, but when I looked again, hoping for at least a little fellow-stranger sympathy, I saw that his brightly colored "hat" was actually a feathery crown. I didn't see many thunderbirds in Chicago, but I knew that their shifted form could be immense, as big as the little room it took me ten seconds to hurry across.

Out in the street, I pulled up my map again and found the quickest way to the museum. *Sergei?*

Woman remained on roof while Galen climbed down. She climbed down when you went inside.

So they were both on the street after me. *Can you see either of them now?*

Galen is finding his way to street you are on. You should be not on it as soon as possible.

Thanks. I strode across the street to an intersection, following the path on my phone as best I could while also getting out of the line of sight of someone coming onto the street.

Sergei kept me posted on Galen's progress, and this time I managed to stay at least two streets ahead of him. Most of the people on the streets avoided me, their keen noses wrinkling at my arrival. Job one would definitely be a bath, once everything else was sorted out.

The Detroit Wolftown Museum, a two-story brick building with a large glass window showing off all the books and plush toys available in their gift shop, thankfully had a large tour group preparing to go in as I arrived.

I snuck in before them and breathed in the cool air-conditioned air of the museum. A uniformed smiling woman came up to me—human form, but probably a wolf. "Good afternoon," she said. "How can—oh, the Community Services building is actually down the street there."

The hitch in that sentence came when she got close enough to smell me. Her nostrils flared—definitely a wolf, or at least an extra with a good nose—but to her credit, she didn't back up a step. I gave her a smile in return and pointed to the group outside. "I'm with a tour group. I just had a kind of," I waved to my clothes, "I fell in some garbage. Could I use the restroom?"

"Oh, of course." She pointed across the lobby to a pair of

doors marked with male and female symbols (rather than human outlines).

"Thanks. Oh, do you have any exhibits on the tunnels under the walls in like the seventies? I'm in graduate school and I'm doing a report on," think think think, "anti-authoritarian movements in minority populations."

"I'm—I think so. But the museum is organized by decade, so if there is, it would be on the second floor in the seventies section." She smiled as the tourist group started to filter in through the doors. "When your group gets up there, we can take a look and see what we have."

If they had anything substantial, she'd know about it. Probably there was a single posterboard or something. "Thanks," I said, and as I headed for the restroom, my phone buzzed.

I picked the non-handicapped stall and sat on the toilet, hoping the buzz was Joelle getting back to me, and thank the heavens above, it was.

Efficient as always, Joelle had called first and then texted when I didn't pick up. She'd written a terse: *wtf!*

You tell me, I wrote back. *In a bathroom, can't talk.*

Prude.

She started typing again, and while she did I typed out quickly, *Also, three warrant officers with guns chasing me, shot at me already.*

The first thing she'd been typing came through first: *There is a warrant in Detroit for you—not Chicago—claims you killed five extras you'd had relationships with. Listed as hate crimes. Obvious bs but how*

And then: *jfc are you ok*

Smell like trash but mostly ok, just want this cleared up.

No shit. I'll make calls, don't know anyone in Detroit so might take a while but getting on it now.

Thanks.

You got a place to hole up?

I think so.

You better know so.

Phone battery ok?

I checked; it was at 53%. *Fine as long as I don't have to use maps too much.*

Stay put then, I'll work on this.

Relief flooded me. It was all going to be okay as long as Galen and his friends couldn't track my garbage scent to the museum. I'd passed a cheap clothing store on the way. Maybe I could slip out, buy a new shirt and pants—and shoes. The docent hadn't noticed my lack of shoes, but someone would.

Sergei, any idea where Galen is?

Three streets over. Still sniffing.

All right, then. New clothes, new smell, and a place to stay hidden while Jo worked on getting the warrant removed. This plan felt better than looking for some ancient, probably nonexistent secret passage out. I slid the phone into my pocket and left the bathroom, stopping at the gift shop to buy a t-shirt that said "Wolftown History" in an elegant font.

CHAPTER 6
SOME THINGS ABOUT GHOSTS

T he clerk at the Boscov's department store clucked sympathetically at my story of having tripped and fallen into a garbage pile. "Let's get you some clean clothes then," he said, ringing up the jacket, pants, socks, and shoes I'd bought. I'd also picked up a pair of cheap sunglasses, hoping it'd make me harder to visually identify.

Sergei thought that was hilarious. Now that we weren't in immediate danger, he reverted to his usual self, meaning that he told me with great relish which sunglasses would make me look "weak," or "like woman" (to his credit, he didn't equate those two, though he did regard them both as insults), and which simply looked, "stupid, like person who live without mirror."

Even when I'd picked out a pair of sunglasses I liked (none of the ones Sergei hated were real options), he laughed. *You think sunglasses will hide you from werewolf's nose?*

Every little bit helps, I told him silently as I paid for my purchases in cash. To the clerk, I asked, "Is there a fitting room or restroom where I can change?"

"Oh, sure." He pointed me to the restroom. "If you're comfortable there."

"Of course," I said. "Thanks so much."

"Stay away from those bins," he said with a smile.

I nodded and went to the restroom to change. My old clothes went into the trash with a little bit of regret; it was a nice shirt and I hated to lose it, but my life was more important now.

You should have bought cologne, Sergei said, which I knew was serious because he thought cologne was disgusting.

Way ahead of you. I walked out past the fragrances department and allowed a slender attractive clerk to spray a sample of cologne onto each wrist. "Very nice," I said, and kept walking out the door.

While I'd been changing, Jo had texted me again. *Recognize any of these names?* She sent five of them along—must be the ones from the warrant. Four of them were unfamiliar, but the fifth...

Yeah, I texted back. *One of them.*

You know, Sergei said as I stared at Czoltan's name on my phone, *I was going to suggest that we go to his house anyway.*

I wouldn't have taken that suggestion. Probably. Maybe I would have. But Czoltan's name on the fake warrant as one of my supposed victims gave me a reason to go see him beyond the ache I still felt from that morning. Come to think of it, he'd appeared just before Galen and Desiree had come out and started shooting at me.

He couldn't be part of it. I mean, I hoped that he didn't hate me enough to want me dead, but more than that, the timing didn't work. The warrant had to have gone up before he'd set out to meet me, and he'd said (and Sergei had confirmed) that Sergei had pushed for the meeting. Even if he and Richard had planned it, what purpose would there be to him showing up at the cafe? To verify that that's where I was? If Richard wanted to do that, he could do it himself, as a ghost. And maybe had; if he could file a fake warrant, I wouldn't bet that Wolftown's ghost security would keep him out.

I looked around. *Sergei, are there any other ghosts around?*

A pause, and then: *None I can detect.*

If Richard were working with Galen, then the warrant wolf would have been a lot better at tracking me. I relaxed, but only a little.

Because I still didn't understand why. I mean, he was a ghost and ghosts did not think the same way we did. How long did it take a ghost to succumb to anxiety spirals and become violent and irrational? Nobody really knew; for obvious reasons there weren't a lot of studies on recent ghosts. The course I'd taken had only said, "After some time," and while there was anecdotal evidence that that time could be as short as a few months, it was usually years.

But if he'd had me right in his house and wanted to kill me, why not do it then? As a ghost, could he have possessed me and made me slit my own throat or something? Possession definitely happened, but not all ghosts knew how or wanted to. Maybe he'd been wary because I have a ghost partner, so he'd assume I knew about ghosts (I do). Or maybe he didn't want Desiree to come home and find my bloody corpse on the kitchen floor. Or he didn't want my ghost to haunt his home.

There was so much I didn't know. Richard must have connections with the Detroit police force or access to their warrant system. When he'd died, something was left undone, and it hit him hard, and it was related to me.

The most traumatic thing Richard had experienced—with

me—had been Breg-lumi. I didn't want to think about that right now. But it was the only thing I could think of that would push him to kill me. We'd gone through it together. Was he afraid I would bring it up again? Was he angry I'd abandoned him to deal with it alone?

When I looked up, feeling I'd taken the line of reasoning as far as I could, I had made it to a street of row homes. The commercial areas of Wolftown lay behind me; here were some of the earlier residential neighborhoods, tightly packed town-homes in earth-toned wood siding and brick, carefully repaired shingle roofs and small porches with plastic chairs and the occasional swing.

Here a human drew more attention. The wolves sitting out on their porches (plus one kishi) watched me as closely as they could without staring. But none of them startled or acted aggressively, so I kept to my walking pace.

The quiet steadiness of this neighborhood calmed me despite my worry that I stood out. As strange as it had felt to be in a bookstore and on a rooftop with a gun aimed at my chest, somehow it felt even less likely that it could happen here. This was where the first wave of werewolf refugees from the Second World War had settled, when people still thought werewolves would want houses just like humans did, without better venti-lation or open spaces. The whole area had a stately, aged charm to it, like an elderly relative who's still extraphobic in little, casual ways. Every time I see the row houses I think of that, how we didn't take the time to ask werewolves how they wanted to live before building houses for them.

I do not think Galen knows where you are, Sergei said. *He is talking on his phone.*

Good. Then Richard isn't helping him find me. I told him briefly what I'd been thinking about. *Can you think of any reason he would have it in for me?*

No. You barely talk to him. A pause. *You barely talk to anybody.*

I go to game night with Joelle and her wife. Which house is Czoltan's?

I didn't need directions, but I wanted Sergei to think I did. He directed me down two streets and over one more, through the older parts of Wolftown Detroit. In Chicago, half the werewolves live close together in that fifteen-story apartment tower and the ones around it; it suits their pack life better and the towers surround a lot of green space.

When I saw the familiar house three porches in from the end of the street, I stopped. In four years, it hadn't changed much. I thought I remembered that the window trim had been white, not reddish-brown; the large pot and Japanese maple on the front porch were also new; a splotch of white paint marred the stone of the first step up to the porch. But the tan/beige siding and brickwork corners, the gutter that ran perfectly straight only to sag at the neighbor's house, and the second-floor window to the bedroom where we'd said good-bye, all those looked exactly as I remembered them from my last look back.

I took a breath and walked up the porch steps.

The door opened before I could knock. I came face to face with a werewolf who was just as startled as I was. Not Czoltan; I realized that in a fraction of a second from his height, his thicker build, and the different shades and patterns of fur on his muzzle and ears, which flattened and then came up again when I didn't pose any immediate threat.

"What?" he said in brash, unaccented English.

"Ah, is Czoltan here?"

His expression relaxed further. "Yeah. Hang on." He leaned back to call into the house. "Hey Zo! Someone at the door." Without waiting for an answer (that I could hear), the werewolf stepped forward and closed the door behind him. "He'll be right down," he told me, and walked past me.

Even though Sergei told me that Galen wasn't anywhere near, I couldn't help looking back to check the street every few seconds. The werewolf who'd opened the door walked away the way I'd come, and I didn't want him to think I was watching him, so I looked the other way, then glanced back that way, and when I turned back to the door there was a wolf's face staring at me through the glass.

I looked back. Czoltan looked the same as he had that morning—as he was leaving annoyed, not as he'd arrived hopeful—and didn't move, just watched me. I couldn't blame him. I didn't know if I'd open the door for me either. So I mouthed the word, "Please."

He rolled his eyes and cracked the door open. "I can hear you through the door, you know."

"I know, but I wanted you to open it."

"What do you want, Jae?"

"Well, uh." A lot of things ran through my head, but honesty seemed the best course. "There's a guy out there who thinks I killed you and a few other werewolves and he wants to shoot me, so I'd like to get out of public streets for a few minutes while my friend Jo tries to sort it out."

His eyes widened and his ears folded flat against his head. "Seriously?"

I held up a hand. "Swear on my father's grave, wherever it is."

He stared at me and I stared back and then he opened the door and stepped aside.

The living room I walked into reminded me of my college apartment, only bigger. Against the back wall, a huge flat-screen TV and larger entertainment unit dominated, facing a wide couch and side table. Two beer cans sat on the side table and one on the carpet at the other end of the couch. The carpet under my new shoes as well as the couch was covered in a fine layer of fur.

Off to my left was the kitchen, and to the far right of the living room, stairs ascended to the second floor. Czoltan made no move to invite me to the couch, nor anywhere else. "How long do you think it'll take?" he asked.

"A couple hours at most. I hope." I tried to give an offhanded casual laugh to show how confident I was that I wouldn't end up dead with a warrant officer's bullets in my heart by the end of the day. From Czoltan's expression, I don't think I pulled it off.

"Okay, well, uh. You want something to drink?"

"Sure."

I followed him to the kitchen. "We don't have a lot of booze," he said. "Sounds like it might be a booze kind of day."

"Maybe after." I grabbed one of the high stools next to the bar at the end of the kitchen and sat down. "Right now just water sounds great."

He took a pitcher from the fridge and a glass from the cupboard. I recognized it: one of the plain pilsner tumblers he'd gotten when he moved in here. His ears flicked as he poured; that meant he was thinking. "So...why does this guy think you killed a bunch of werewolves? And why me?"

"That's a complicated question," I said. "The easy part is that there's a warrant out for my arrest on five counts of murder, the motive being that I apparently hate werewolves who, uh." I'd started that sentence without thinking about where it would end, but now I was stuck. "Are in relationships with humans."

His eyebrows rose as he placed the glass in front of me. "Are, or were?"

I hadn't thought I was thirsty, but as soon as I started

drinking, I couldn't stop until the whole glass was drained. I set it back down on the bar. "They claimed you were dead, so I'm thinking they're not big on accuracy."

He took the glass and refilled it.

"Are you?" I asked as he set it back down in front of me.

"Big on accuracy?"

"In a relationship with a human?"

To refill the pitcher, he had to face away from me at the sink. I only heard water running, and then it stopped. He replaced the pitcher in the fridge, took out a can of sparkling water, and let the door swing shut. "No," he said, and faced me. "Are you?"

The glass of water felt cool to my fingers. I left my hands wrapped around it and shook my head. "No. Just a ghost."

"What?" That startled him enough to bristle his tail.

"Sergei," I said. "You met him?"

"The bear?" He rubbed his ears when I nodded. "Right. I didn't realize he was—you were—"

Tell him it is not romantic, Sergei insisted.

"It's not romantic," I said.

Czoltan's ears splayed out to the sides. "I didn't think it was. I mean, how would that even—"

"There are people who have romantic relationships with ghosts," I said. "Don't judge. But me and Sergei, we're just friends."

And business partners.

"And business partners."

Even though you take all the money.

"And sometimes he interferes in my non-business life."

Czoltan accepted this. He took a drink of his sparkling water. "So why is there a fake warrant out on you that says you killed me? Seems too specific to be a glitch in the system."

Glitch in the system. That was a good English slang phrase.

"I'm still trying to figure that out. I'm pretty sure I know who, but I still can't figure out why."

"Weird. Are you sure they're trying to kill you?"

"Well," I said, "I've been shot at several times and chased through Wolftown and I jumped off a roof into a dumpster and had to buy a whole new outfit today."

His ears went all the way back and his eyes widened. He put his glass of water down and it clattered on the counter; his paw was shaking. "Oh shit, Jae, are you serious?"

"Yeah," I said, and brushed fingers down my shirt. "It's okay, I didn't like the other clothes that much."

He half-laughed and took a step toward me. "You've been shot at?"

"They showed up right after you left." I gave him a quick summary of the morning's events. "The other shirt had a rip in it, but I threw that out, so I guess I can't prove it."

That half-laugh came up again as I described the rooftop standoff. "You were cornered on a roof and jumped into a dumpster?"

I pulled up my sleeve to show him the scrape, and then my pant leg to show where my shin had hit the metal. "There's not really a bruise there yet, but it hurts."

"It's red, I can see." He reached out, then withdrew his paw. "You're sure you're not in a movie and nobody told you?"

I rubbed the bruise. "I'm just glad to have a safe place to rest for a little while."

"Of course," he said, and this time he did rest a paw on my wrist. His fingers felt good and the warmth untwisted something in me.

"I wanted to say something earlier," I said all in a rush. "I'm sorry."

"It's okay." He left his fingers there on my skin. "What did you want to say?"

120

"That. That I'm sorry. But also I'm sorry about earlier. Sergei can show me things and he was showing me Richard's wife, right as I was trying to talk to you."

Czoltan looked around the room as though Sergei were in the kitchen with us, which he might have been. He was being very quiet. "He can show you things?"

"Our minds are linked. That's what it means to bind a ghost."

"So he's, like, a slave?"

I like this one.

"Binding gives ghosts a structure. Without a binding, a lot of them become very focused on their own emotions and can do damage to other people. Having a non-ghost mind to bind to keeps them linked to the real world and gives them 'empathetic grounding,' they call it."

This theory requires that binding mind also be grounded.

Czoltan's fingers lifted, leaving colder air on my skin. In reflexive reaction to losing that connection, pushed by the desire I'd had to feel his fur again, I flipped my hand over and brushed fingers against his wrist before he could move very far. I wasn't holding him, but he let his paw remain there. "I don't know much about ghosts."

My fingers rubbed his fur. I'd dated one or two werewolves in the four years since Czoltan, but there was something about his fur and scent that still pulled at memories like threads in my mind, bringing up connections I'd buried. "They died with unfinished business, something that ties their spirit to this world so strongly that they can't let go."

The wolf nodded. His fingers curled and claws barely touched my arm. "So what's Sergei's deal?"

Do you mind?

Bah. She is dead one hundred years, what harm?

"He had a fight with his wife, left to go raid a village, and was killed. He never got to tell her he loves her again, and her last memory of him will be the fight."

"Oh. That sucks." Czoltan's ears went back. "Couldn't he just go tell her after he died, when he was a ghost?"

"Sometimes, but unfortunately by the time he'd figured out ghost things, the village he'd been raiding had found his home and retaliated for the ones he'd killed by killing the people there, including his wife."

"Ah, shit. Is he here?" The wolf looked around. "I'm sorry, man. That's horrible."

I nodded. "He says thank you."

I did not.

You should have.

"Anyway, so he was haunting Russia and being generally pretty out of control, and a ghost dealer captured him."

Czoltan broke in. "What does 'out of control' mean? Did he kill anyone?"

Sergei remained silent. "I don't know," I lied. "Being bound is sort of like...being born again, I guess. So I don't know much about his unbound life."

"Were you the first one to bind him?"

I shook my head. "He was bound a couple other times, but his owners died or gave him up. He didn't last long with either, and I don't know a lot about them."

You have not asked. They were boring. Never jumped off roof.

"But he and I have gotten along pretty well over the years."

Czoltan's eye came to rest on my other hand, the one with the ring. He nodded toward it. "He's in there?"

"Kind of."

"And if you take it off...?"

"The binding stays. But he can't communicate with me the way he can when I wear it."

The claws slid forward on my skin and the soft pads of his

fingers brushed my arm. "Is there any way he can let go? Stop being a ghost?"

I nodded. "There are banishment spells, but—"

But it is like being pushed off roof instead of taking stairs. Maybe you land in garbage.

You don't know that.

You don't know it is not that.

I sighed. "They feel violent and there's no guarantee that they allow the spirit to go to the same place. Nobody's ever come back from it, but some ghosts don't trust the banishment spells. So they stay."

Czoltan nodded. "I get that." He scanned the kitchen again and raised his voice. "It's uh, the same with extras, kind of. There's things you can take to control your behavior out among the norms, but...they make you feel weird."

Should I speak to him directly?

Not right now.

Aloud, I said, "It's kind of the same thing. I mean, more extreme."

"Sure, I get that." He'd perked his ears, and when Sergei didn't respond, he relaxed them. "I feel bad for him. I wish there was a way to put ghosts to rest peacefully."

Our fingers and arms had been resting against each other for a while. "Yeah," I said. "I know what you mean."

We stayed there for a second, and then a few more while I tried to sort out my feelings and my situation, all of which were jostling for space in my thoughts as the presence of my ex and his fingers on my skin were rapidly constricting the amount of available thinking space. I would think, *I should check to see if Jo texted me*, followed by, *Why would Richard want to kill me?* And then, *I'm sure I've read about something called an "old times' sake fuck," haven't I*, followed by, *Don't be an ass.*

123

Most of this was kept private from Sergei, but he's no fool. *Do not fuck him if you plan to walk away again,* he told me.

I'm not. But Christ.

Not planning to fuck him or not planning to walk away again?

I don't know! I can't—

"What's he saying?" Czoltan asked, not smiling but not angry.

"He's saying he likes you," I blurted out.

"Maybe I can talk to him sometime."

Now?

Not yet.

"Sometime, sure." I touched the scrape on my elbow. "Hey, do you have any bandages around? Some antiseptic maybe?"

"It's, uh, upstairs in the bathroom."

Werewolves healed pretty quickly. They'd use antiseptic on cuts, but between the healing and the fur, they almost never used bandages. Which meant that Czoltan still had bandages from when we'd been going out.

Smooth, Sergei said dryly.

Shut up.

If you fuck him, I will not watch.

I'm not going to—I needed a bandage.

Which you knew was upstairs.

Sometimes people keep bandages in the kitchen.

"Do you mind? I'd really appreciate it."

"Yeah, no problem." Czoltan got up—his fingers leaving my arm—and then paused. "Why don't you come upstairs too? You could wash that off."

I tried very hard not to look at the kitchen sink. "If you're sure."

"Yeah." His muzzle broke into a smile, and his tail flicked with what I was pretty sure was a restrained wag. "Come on."

I followed that tail up the narrow carpeted stair. *You're just getting a bandage*, I told myself. *Nothing's changed between you.* Well—that wasn't true. Nothing had changed in me; that was the problem.

The smells at the top of the stairs were strong, and not just of wolf. Czoltan's cologne, mild downstairs, accumulated up here where he put it on, where he discarded his clothes, where he slept. Immersed in it, I remembered the pain of breaking up, but also the good times prior to that. The best times were when we felt that we were the only people in the world and nobody else mattered, but that wasn't reality. Reality lay in wait just outside, always ready with a stray bomb to blow your little world apart. Better to separate before those bombs could fall.

And yet, and yet, and yet, I'd almost died out there today. Could've been shot by a warrant officer, could've missed the dumpster jumping off the roof, could've contracted a disease from garbage (still waiting on that one). I hadn't really processed it, focused on staying alive and ahead of Galen, but now, safe, my body relaxed and my mind went into overdrive.

We'd just been talking about ghosts, about Sergei and the longing that had kept him in this world, and my mind jumped on those tracks and chugged along with every step I took. If I'd died, would there be anything strong enough to keep me in this world? I wasn't sure, but if there were, the smart money favored the wolf standing at the bathroom door gesturing me in.

Putting someone out of your life for four years doesn't put them out of your mind. When you discover that they haven't moved on either, that they still have memories of you around, and that they're willing to take you in (granted, things would have to be bad for them to say "get back out onto the street where someone's trying to murder you," but still), those memories of the breakup come back. It was harder to remember the resolve I felt, the fear that my family would break us up, the necessity of doing it, and easier to remember how difficult the words had been to force past my throat, how hard Czoltan had tried to hold back tears, how awkwardly I'd left the room for the last time, wanting to hug him but instead leaving him standing next to the bed (that bed, the one I could see through the open bedroom door, the sheets rumpled as they always were because he couldn't be bothered to make his bed ever).

And when I went into the bathroom, he started running water. "Roll up your sleeve," he instructed. I complied, watching his muzzle as I did. His ears and eyes, focused on the task, betrayed no emotion.

I couldn't very well ask, "hey, are you thinking about our breakup too?" So I extended my arm for him to dab at it with a washcloth, then carefully spread antiseptic cream on it, and finally pick apart a bandage and cover the wound. I could've managed it myself, but he didn't ask and I didn't insist.

"Anywhere else?" he asked when I'd rolled down my shirt sleeve.

I shook my head. "A bunch of bruises, but nothing to do about those. I don't think anything's broken, miracle of miracles."

"You might have a hairline fracture in your leg. You should get it x-rayed to be sure."

I exhaled. "I should. Maybe when this is all over."

"Any word from your friend?"

I checked my phone. "Not yet."

Czoltan gestured to the bathroom door. "I guess you're here for a while longer."

We walked out into the hallway and stood there. The options were to go into the bedroom or go back downstairs, but when I hesitated to see which one he would pick, he leaned against the wall next to the bathroom door and stuck his paws into his pockets.

"Listen," I said. "I really am sorry. I tried to say that earlier and got sidetracked."

His ears went back and he looked away, at the bedroom and then at the stairs. "You don't have to."

"I know I don't have to. But I feel bad about—"

"Oh, do you?" Now he looked at me. "Do you feel bad?"

"I—"

"You don't get to feel bad," he said. "You're the one who broke up. You got what you wanted."

"I didn't—" I cut myself off, Czoltan staring at me.

"You didn't what? Didn't want to? Too bad. You did it, you have to live with it, and you don't get to feel bad about it." He jabbed a claw at his chest. "*I* feel bad. I'm allowed to. I let you in here anyway, I bandaged you up because I don't want you to die, but I don't have to listen to you whine about how you feel bad about—about whatever."

That felt worse than falling into the dumpster. "You're right," I said. "But I was just going to say I was sorry about imposing on you like this."

His ears came up a bit and he squinted at me. "Really?"

"Uh...I am sorry about that. But no, you were right. I was going to apologize for—" I looked at the bedroom. "But—no, I guess I shouldn't."

"I said you can't feel bad." Czoltan folded his arms. "I didn't say you can't apologize."

"All right, well. I'm sorry. I really am."

He kept staring at me, so after a moment I went on. "For breaking up with you. And for the way it came sort of out of nowhere, I guess. I mean, things had been going pretty well. Really well. And then..." I scratched my head. "Look, I don't want to relive it."

TIM SUSMAN

"Me neither. But it's good to hear you apologize."

I gave him a half-smile. "Yeah, I—"

"I don't accept it." He walked to the bedroom door. "Help yourself to more water in the kitchen. Let yourself out when it's safe."

The door closed, leaving me in the hallway. I took a step toward it, first to open it, then to knock, but I did neither of those things. I waited, knowing he could hear when I went downstairs, and when he didn't come out again I descended the narrow staircase to the kitchen.

Jo still hadn't texted. I kept checking my phone anyway, as if it wouldn't buzz with a text message. It was hard not to text her again; she knew the urgency and was working on it. Bothering her wasn't going to help.

So I got a glass of water and sat at the counter again, thinking about relationships and family and ghosts. Sergei became visible and stood across from me. "It is good that you apologized."

"It doesn't feel good."

"Not to you. But you did the wrong."

"It wasn't—" I took a drink of water and calmed myself. "It was necessary."

He folded his arms. "I am still not convinced of this."

"You know my mother."

"Your mother wants you to have relationship. You think she would not be happy with relationship here? She did not like Czoltan?"

I rubbed my eyes. "You know how she is with extras."

"Ah. You never tried."

"What would be the use of that?" Aware that I was raising my voice, I tried to lower it, with not a lot of success.

Sergei shrugged his massive shoulders. "She might surprise you. Maybe things are different now."

128

"Did you hear her talk about Wolftown? Every time I talk about doing work there?"

"So you decided that happiness was not worth the risk."

I shook my head. "You've been pining after your wife for a century. I would think you'd be down on relationships."

He smiled. "I have felt the true power of love, and you have not. Love," he spread his arms, "keeps me here."

"I've felt it," I protested. "I mean, maybe. I just didn't have the person I loved die."

The floor overhead creaked. I listened for the latch of the bedroom door, but didn't hear it. And then my mind snapped some pieces together. The person I loved, and dying, and Sergei and what was keeping him here. "Oh, shit," I said.

Sergei glanced at me curiously. "Only now you see what you have thrown away?"

"No," I breathed. "I think I know why Richard put up that fake warrant."

"Why?" Sergei couldn't hide his interest even as he tried to deflect it. "It was something you said to him, was it not?"

"No. I mean, I don't think so. I think he wasn't trying to kill *me*. When I saw Desiree in the bookstore, she was sweating. I didn't think much of it because, well, I was too."

"She was chasing you."

I nodded. "I know. I could be wrong. I haven't seen it in years. But that could also be the early stages of K-118 poisoning."

"Why does Richard want to kill his wife? You said he loves her."

"He does." I shook my head. "I know it doesn't sound logical, but it has to do with this town, Breg-lumi. Richard and I were there in Kosovo and it was—it was fucked up. That whole war was fucked up, but that town..."

Sergei waited, and when I didn't go on, he prodded me. "What happened in this Breg-lumi?"

I could've just shared the memories with him. But I'd spent years not thinking about it, and to uncover all of it at once would have been bad for both of us, I thought. If I verbalized, at least I could control how he—and I—experienced it here. It moved it out of the realm of my mind and gave me some distance.

"Breg-lumi was a town not too far from Klina, on the White River. Breg-lumi means "Riverside." There was one beautiful old stone bridge, and white houses with red tile roofs, flower gardens, even a little fountain in the town square. There was another town named Breg-lumi a few miles away, and so this one didn't get put on the maps because people thought there was only one. Anyway, the Serbian army had passed it by and all of these things were undamaged when we got there." I stopped to picture it. Part of the horror of it had been coming along the bend in the road and seeing Breg-lumi lying there in the sun like a painting. We hadn't believed that anything bad could happen there.

"Because it had escaped harm, it had become a kind of secondary refugee camp, and about a hundred people holed up there. A lot of the time when families got separated, some of them would end up in our camp and we wouldn't know where the others had gotten to. We heard about this town through an underground network, and the KLA—the Kosovo Liberation Alliance—hadn't told us about it, so we did a couple recons, low-key, and found it.

"The woman who told us about it, Manjola, was certain her husband had gone there. There were half a dozen others, men and women, whose spouses or partners or children or parents had gone there, they were certain. We didn't tell them otherwise, but we were cautious until our surveillance came back and told us that yes, there was a town, and yes, there were people.

"Richard headed up the team to go get these refugees and bring them back to our camp. Sure, Breg-lumi—this one— wasn't on maps, but it was very vulnerable, and we had—we had spies, we knew, refugees and workers who were sympathetic to the Serbian side. So as soon as we knew, there was a ticking clock to when they would know.

"And yeah, you can see where this is all going. We got there, everything looked great. We stopped to send a couple people ahead, recon again to make sure it wasn't a trap. While they were scouting, we got an urgent call that told us to pull back, that the Serbian army had bombers on the way, and even though our drab junker buses didn't look like targets, they wouldn't protect us much if they were in the line of fire. We had an armed escort, but no anti-aircraft batteries.

"Our locals looking for their families wanted to run in and save them, and some of us wanted to do that too. But Richard did the right thing. He and I took a bullhorn and went ahead, just the two of us, trying to get close enough to warn the town. We didn't have a siren or anything, and when he yelled from the busses' location nobody responded.

"We'd gotten to the hill overlooking the bridge when we heard the bombers. If we'd come in with the busses, we'd all be easy targets, so again, Richard was smart here. Right around then we finally got a response to the bullhorn. Some people by the bridge heard us yell that they were in danger, in our limited Albanian, but instead of running toward us—to safety—they ran back into the town."

Sergei spoke for the first time. "To save their friends."

"To save their friends." I sighed. "And from the time you hear the bombers to the time the bombs fall is... five minutes maybe?"

"So they died in the bombs."

"No. As it happened. Some of them did, but the refugees weren't the target of the bombers. It turned out the KLA had been using one of the buildings in the town as munitions storage. The Serbians got a few civilian casualties but most of the strike was centered on the munitions. They didn't want us to find and take them."

"And they..." Sergei mimed an explosion.

I nodded. "But you remember that K-118 I was mentioning? The bioweapon? The thing that accelerates people's metabolism until they die? Well. There was some of that there. It doesn't survive long out in the air, but with a strong dispersal force—like a bunch of other munitions exploding—it can get pretty far before it decomposes. So basically almost anyone in that town who wasn't killed by the bombs was exposed. And of course," I pinched my eyes shut, "of course they were running. They were terrified."

"Of course." Sergei sounded tired.

"They got all the way across that stone bridge, a lot of them," I said. "Up to where we were, and we guided them back to the busses. We didn't know about the K-118 then. We thought we were getting them away. Of course they were sweating; they were terrified, running as fast as they could.

"We got them almost all the way to the busses before the first ones dropped.

"Still, we didn't know. We just thought, you know, fear and seizures. The first ones to go were children, and it was only two of them. Richard and I carried them back to the bus.

"But they were dead before we got on the bus. And over the next hour, more of them died.

"The trip back to our camp was a four hour ride. Only one of the refugees managed to die in our camp."

I didn't want to talk about the reunions on the bus, people

meeting long-lost family members and then having to watch them die. Or the people who didn't have anyone to meet, who were just grateful for escape, who died alone. Richard and I and others would sit with them, once we understood what was going on, but we found several curled up in seats, already dead, staring blankly at the seat ahead of them with nobody at their side.

"This is not war." Sergei's voice was flat. "To kill a man without looking into his eyes? To kill children? This is cowardice."

"It's what we've turned war into."

He snorted. "You believe that because Richard lived through this horror that he would want to inflict it on his wife?"

"I believe that ghost-Richard would." I met Sergei's eyes.

After a moment, he looked away. "Perhaps. *Da.*"

"More than that, though. We went back to Breg-lumi later that week. Not all the K-118 was destroyed. We collected a bunch of the canisters and brought them to the U.N. authorities. There wasn't ever a specific count, though. One or two could have gone into Richard's pack and none of us would ever have known."

"You never told me about that." The voice wasn't Sergei's; it came from the stair.

I looked up and saw Czoltan stepping down from the shadows. "Sorry," he said. "There's a vent in the kitchen—I could hear what you were saying."

"It's all right," I said. "I didn't want to tell you about it."

"I knew the people from Breg-lumi got killed, but I thought you'd just brought them back to bury them."

"That's the story we told. The KLA was still denying that it used K-118 and there was a chance that the Serbs had dropped it with the bombs. We had to go back later to confirm."

"There must have been many ghosts created that day," Sergei said quietly.

"Probably." I rubbed my eyes. "I don't know. I didn't know how to find them then. The U.N. has a thing against it to stop people from collecting up wartime ghosts and..." I exhaled.

Czoltan crossed the kitchen. "So you think Richard used K-118 on Desiree? Doesn't that mean that you should be hurrying?"

CHAPTER 7
EXIGENT
CIRCUMSTANCES

" Of course we should hurry," I said. "This was about an hour ago, so she has anywhere between zero and a couple hundred minutes left."

"If you're right."

"She was sweating so much. I was running for my life and I wasn't sweating that much. But yeah, fine. Sergei!" The bear turned to me. "Go find Desiree. If she's suffering from K-118, she'll be..." The people on the bus looked up at me, sweating, bodies jerking. "Agitated, clutching her chest maybe, breathing hard. She might look like she's having a seizure. They had convulsions in the last fifteen-twenty minutes."

He nodded quickly and then disappeared. Czoltan waited a moment and then descended the stairs to the other side of the kitchen from me. "So you think her husband used this extremely rare bioweapon on his wife, why exactly? As punishment for cheating?"

"I think he wanted to kill her so they could be ghosts together," I said. "Or something like that. He's a ghost so his actions are driven almost entirely by emotion rather than reason."

"All right." Czoltan rubbed his muzzle. "And if it is that, then what's the cure?"

"There's—one cure." He raised an eyebrow, so I took a breath and told him. "It doesn't work on werewolves. Metabolism's too different. So if she gets bitten..."

"Whoa, wait," the wolf said. He held his paws up. "There's —that's so illegal."

"Not in the case where the person's life is in danger and the change could save her." I got up. "Do you still keep the wolfs-bane..." I opened the cabinet over the sink and got up on the counter to reach into the top shelf.

"Hey!" Czoltan hurried over to push me away, but I'd already found the small metal tin. "That's—my roommate must have—"

"Doesn't matter." I slid off the counter and pressed the box into his paw. "This will save a life."

"Look." He weighed the tin. "They're not going to believe me either."

"I'll go with you. I can explain it all."

"Aren't you hiding here because people want to shoot you?"

"Yes, and how would I feel if Desiree died because I played it safe?"

Czoltan shook his head. "There's playing it safe and then there's being an idiot and getting yourself killed."

"Hold on. Do you know Galen?" He shook his head slowly. "What about—Sergei, did we ever get the name of that other officer, the woman?"

"No."

"I have one friend who's a warrant officer," Czoltan said. "Or, not a friend really, but at least he knows me."

"Call him," I said. "Have him look up the warrant so he can see you're listed as a victim. Then he'll know it's fake. Maybe he can—I don't know, send something out or something so Galen will know not to shoot me."

Jae, Sergei said. *I have found them. Desiree is not well.* He showed me Desiree, sitting on the sidewalk, dripping sweat and panting. Galen stood over her with a paw on her shoulder and his helpless terror ripped at my heart.

"Shit," I said aloud. "Sergei says Desiree looks really bad. She's not convulsing yet though."

The wolf took his phone out. "Do you really think there's a chance we can save her?"

"There's definitely a chance." Okay, she'd believed I was a serial killer, but Desiree was a good person and didn't deserve —no, don't think about the bus. We're in a city of werewolves. We can save her if we act fast.

"All right." He dialed.

Fast doesn't mean stupid. Getting an officer to acknowledge that the warrant was fake didn't require much more proof than the appearance, alive, of one of the supposed victims. Getting anyone to believe that a werewolf's bite was Desiree's only chance of survival would take a bit more.

While Czoltan called his friend, I tried to find anything on the web about K-118. Ideally, you know, it would be a single page that anyone could read in about thirty seconds that would exactly describe Desiree's symptoms, convey the immediate danger, and recommend transition as the only remedy.

Of course, nothing like what you need exists unless you've written it yourself. The Wikipedia entry was a bare, "K-118 was a biochemical weapon allegedly used in the Second Kosovo War.[citation needed]" I got a little more off a military site listing banned substances, and finally the best I found was a blog by some veteran of the war talking about a K-118 attack I

137

had only heard about. It didn't sound quite as bad as Breg-lumi, but then, not much did. The blog had the benefit of also explaining that K-118 had been developed for assassinations because it so closely mimicked a heart attack.

Sergei reappeared in the kitchen while I was doing my research, startling Czoltan into an exclamation on his call. He glared at the bear as he hung up. "My buddy doesn't know Galen, but there's a warrant officer board he can post to. He said it would be best if he meets us there."

"That's fantastic. Thank him for us."

"So, uh." He held his phone, turning to Sergei and back to me. "Where is 'there'?"

"Right. Sergei, can you make sure the street outside is clear?"

The bear sighed and vanished. *Always the same*, he said in my head. *Sergei, go do my job for me.*

I took his renewed complaints as a positive sign and ignored them. "We can get going in a second," I told Czoltan.

Saving Desiree was important, but I realized that once we were done with that, I might not see Czoltan again. He was looking at me with more tenderness than he had all day, and that pulled at my heart even as my head yelled that this was not the time.

Czoltan must have been feeling the same thing. He set his phone down on the kitchen counter and nodded. "Sorry about...blowing up at you."

"Don't be. I deserve it. And you've been waiting years to say it."

That brought a small smile to his lips. "Still. It didn't feel as good as I imagined it would in my head."

"Those things rarely do." I steepled my fingers together and rested my chin on them. "I really appreciate you helping us out. I wouldn't have blamed you if you wanted to stay upstairs."

"I did kind of want to," he admitted. "But on balance I would prefer that you not get shot."

"Me too."

He was right across the counter from me, his nose less than a foot from mine. I put my hands down halfway between us on the cool smooth surface. He didn't move his paws at all. "What's it like, having someone in your head all the time?"

"He's not in my head all the time. It's like a relationship, I guess, except it's easier to communicate."

His ears went back and he looked down. "I guess I can see that. You can't really get away from each other."

"Not really. I know of some people who hate their bound ghosts, but the ghosts are useful and it costs too much to switch, so they're stuck with them. I got lucky with Sergei, but really, I think most ghosts are pretty reasonable once they're bound. After all, they're anchored to the world through you, so —well, there's theories that if you hate your bound ghost, it means you hate a part of yourself."

"Oh, weird. So, like, they're partly you?"

"Partly."

He studied the counter surface, carefully not meeting my eyes. "Does that make it hard to go on dates?"

I raised an eyebrow. "Do you want to talk about dates?"

Now he looked up and half-smiled. "In the abstract, I guess."

"Well, there are things I can shut off from him. And Sergei can 'go away' for a bit so I can have private times, though he can also come back without my permission. He's annoyingly interested in—you know, 'private' times. Even though he's not gay."

The wolf grimaced. "So it's like having a roommate and a door that doesn't lock."

"Yeah, kind of. He keeps pushing me to date."

"Does he judge your dates? Tari—my roommate—he brings his dates over before they go out and then he asks my opinion of them."

The conversation felt inane when Desiree might be dying out there, and yet there was nothing else to do right now. And Czoltan was important too. This conversation had been too long delayed. Still, I should check in. *Sergei?* I asked.

I am searching all the streets between here and there. Mistake means you get shot. You wish I should hurry?

"He does judge them," I said, "but mostly he likes them more than I do."

"You shouldn't date someone if you don't like them."

I thought perhaps he was teasing me, because his ears were still up and he was still half-smiling. "Sometimes it's not about liking," I said. "But most of them are perfectly nice. Sometimes they turn out not to be gay."

"Hah," he snorted. "I had that happen once."

"So awkward."

He nodded. "I felt like asking someone to dinner was a clue that it was a date, but I guess straight guys do that with each other now too?"

"Seems that way. Anyway, they were all mostly fine. Just, you know." It was harder to look at him. "They weren't right."

We sat in silence until Czoltan said, "So, nothing from Sergei yet?"

"Not yet."

"Can't you see what he's seeing?"

"If I wanted to or asked him to share it. Right now I don't care until he gives us the all-clear."

"Oh."

And we sat there again, in silence. I should be fidgety, antsy to get out the door, but that understanding was detached from my focus on Czoltan. The thing I'd been worried about upon seeing him again wasn't that he'd hate me. I'd really been worried that he wouldn't care. If he'd moved on, that would be one thing; if he'd pushed away the emotions and replaced me, if he still loved but had found someone better and more worthy of it, I'd be sad—

(wait, what?)

—but I'd be happy for him. But if he were indifferent, if he didn't care at all, if he remembered me only as an unfortunate episode in his life the way he might have remembered a job he'd held for a couple months, that would've hurt me more than anything.

He wasn't indifferent. He was mad, after four years. He'd held on to the thing he'd wanted to say to me. And when he'd heard me talking about Breg-lumi, he'd come down. It had touched him.

The thing I hadn't been afraid of was that I would feel indifferent. I knew how I felt. I knew it would be a mistake to do anything about it, but I also knew it was hurting too much not to. If Sergei had been there and not searching Wolftown, he might've told me not to slide off my stool and walk around the end of the counter. He might've told me to stop at the point where I reached out for Czoltan's paws. He might've groaned an old Russian curse when I leaned forward.

Then again, he might not have.

But I know for sure he would have shut up when we kissed.

It was one of those kisses where you both know it's going to happen. Maybe both of you know it shouldn't, but neither of you is going to stop it. His lips were as warm as I remembered, his scent a little different, but the feel of him, those wolf's lips and sharp teeth against my tongue, was just the same as if it were four years ago again and I was greeting him when he came over to visit. His whiskers tickled my face and he made a small humming noise as we kissed, bringing his paws up to my shoulders.

Even though I'd initiated it, even though he'd yelled at me just a few minutes ago, we both sank into the kiss like we were holding onto each other alone in an ocean. I put my hands on his ribs and they felt a little different in a way I wasn't really focused on quantifying.

Holding each other while we kissed felt good, really good. The kiss turned greedy as we went from tentatively getting to know each other again to not wanting it to end. Finally, we broke apart and rested together like that, nose to nose, me looking down the long bridge of his muzzle to his greenish-brown eyes.

"Sorry," he said softly.

"Sorry?" I laughed.

"Yeah." His eyes flicked to one side but couldn't stay away for long. "I just had to know."

"If I still..."

"No." His breath warmed my chin. "If *I* still cared. Your scent hit me with a lot."

"I guess we both do," I said, and bit back any further words.

Your path is clear.

The knowledge that this reunion would fade didn't make it feel any less warm. Nor did the awareness that I had a more urgent job to do than kissing my ex. "You know I didn't break up with you because I didn't love you."

"Yeah, I know." His ears stayed up. "It's been so hard to let go of you, though. I think I wished I wouldn't feel anything when I smelled you. When I talked to you."

"Sergei says it's clear." I didn't let him go. "We should get going, I guess."

"Yeah." He didn't let go either.

Jae! She needs attention!

I winced and pulled my hands back. "All right, we should —let's go. Tell your friend to meet us."

Where? I asked back.

Finally, he grumbled. *Were you fucking him?*

No. He kissed me.

Hmph. Come to Merchant and Droszny.

"Merchant and Droszny," I relayed. "And hurry, Sergei says she's not doing well."

"Ah, shit." Czoltan pulled out his phone and typed. I did love how seriously he was taking this, how much the welfare of this woman he barely knew mattered to him. He waited a moment. "All right, he says he's on his way."

"We should get close by to be ready. Bring the wolfsbane." I gathered up my phone. "I'm glad you're coming along."

"I am too." He smiled. Everything was the way it used to be.

(Only it wasn't, and I knew it wasn't, but for the moment that didn't matter, and the part of my brain that should've told me otherwise remained silent.)

His friend said he'd text when he was there. Sergei gave us more details of the scene: Desiree was on her back on the sidewalk now, Galen tending to her and thinking she'd had a heart attack. Paramedics had arrived in a small electric vehicle, but they hadn't loaded her onto it yet. *If they try to move her, you have to stop them,* I told him.

I will do whatever I can, he promised.

And tell me if she starts convulsing.

Czoltan and I hurried without running. A human with a werewolf attracted less attention than a human alone in this part of town, but with my mind on Desiree, I didn't even worry about the curious glances. He kept checking his phone; we didn't want to arrive before his friend did.

"What does your roommate do?" I asked, to make conversation.

"Call center. That's where I met him. It was nice to meet someone who didn't have any connection, you know, to older stuff."

"Oh, was he born here?"

Czoltan nodded. "Grandparents came over after World War II. His parents actually worked in one of the suburbs, I forget which one. Deer Park or something. Still live there. But he moved back to Wolftown because he hated high school. Being an extra in a mostly-human school, people called him 'monster' and stuff like that."

"Shit."

"Yeah. One kid tried to shake his hand with a silver ring once, but his friends stopped him." The wolf rubbed his paws. "At least it was a decent neighborhood and that was all they did physically. You heard about that kid in Utah a few years ago?"

I nodded. "That was messed up."

"Yeah. Anyway, Tari got tired of it and moved here a couple years ago. He was staying in an apartment when I met him at the call center. I think the hardest thing for him was..." Czoltan gestured to himself. "Going around like we do here. He stayed human most of his life, and it feels...like going out naked, he says. But I guess if everyone else is 'naked' too then it doesn't matter as much."

"I can see that. He seemed pretty well-adjusted from the ten seconds I saw him."

"Yeah, he's cool."

"You didn't date?"

"Nah, he's straight. Sometimes, you know, if it's just us and we're, uh." He fingered the tin of wolfsbane in his pocket. "We'll, like, cuddle up on the couch. It's nice."

I briefly wondered whether I would have cuddled up with Sergei if it had been an option. Even if he could become corporeal, he probably would not have been interested. The thought reminded me to check in with him. *How is it going?*

They are not moving her, he replied tersely. *She is still.*

"He's pretty secure in his sexuality, I guess."

"Seems to be. I offered to do stuff with him once and he said no, and it was all cool."

"Kids these days."

Czoltan nodded. "They're lucky."

"In some ways."

His paw grasped my hand. "In a lot of the ways that matter."

It seemed to be taking Czoltan's friend an awful long time to get there. We were a block away and there was still no word from him. At the space between two townhouses, Czoltan and I stopped and rested against cool bricks in shadow. It was at that moment that Sergei said, *She has started to convulse.*

I pushed away memories and took a breath. "We're going to have to go now," I said. "We can't wait for your friend."

Czoltan grabbed my wrist. "He'll shoot you."

"Not if you go out first." His concern warmed me. I put my hand over his paw, the soft fur and warm love below it. "Tell him there isn't much time left."

"Maybe I can convince him to bite her." Czoltan took the

tin of wolfsbane out of his pocket. "He doesn't need to see you at all."

"You can try," I said.

I can help, Sergei added.

"But," I went on, "I don't know how a warrant officer will react to a stranger coming up to tell him to illegally bite someone on the street."

"How will he react to someone he thinks is a serial killer?" Czoltan pocketed the tin again and bent to kiss my forehead. "All right, I'm going."

"Sergei will help," I called after him as he walked down the street. He raised a paw to indicate he'd heard, and then turned the corner.

Sergei, let me see, I told him, moving farther back into shadow and closing my eyes.

My view switched in time to see Czoltan coming around the corner, jogging and then pushing his way through the small crowd that had formed. Two paramedics, a wolf and a huli jing, knelt over Desiree, one holding her while the other stopped her from swallowing her tongue. Galen stood nearby, shifting from one foot to the other. The confident warrant officer who'd faced me in the bookstore and on the roof was now a worried wolf watching his lover die.

My chest tightened. The murmurs of the crowd, the low words the paramedics were saying to each other, everything faded behind the roar in my ears. I couldn't close Sergei's eyes, so I had to keep watching the scene, watching as the fox-woman injected something into Desiree's arm. It might slow the symptoms, but unless they had access to some military biotech that had been developed in the last seven years, it wasn't going to stop the process.

"I know what's wrong with her." Czoltan pushed through the crowd and came to stand beside Galen.

"She's having a heart attack," Galen said tightly, and turned slightly to face Desiree and put his shoulder to Czoltan.

"No." Czoltan stepped around Galen, coming very close to stepping on Desiree's leg.

"Hey." The wolf paramedic stood up and held her paws out. "Both of you keep back, please."

"She's been poisoned with an old military bioweapon," Czoltan said. "It's Serbian, called K-eighteen."

One-eighteen, I thought, but there was no way to correct him and it wouldn't matter anyway.

"The only way to save her is for a werewolf to bite her," Czoltan went on.

"All right, all right." The wolf paramedic stepped around Galen and took Czoltan's arm. "Let's go, we're trying to save a life here."

"So am I!" he yelled, resisting.

Galen didn't say anything, but thanks to Sergei I heard the huli jing say, "Damn biters."

"Just stand back, please, sir." The wolf paramedic's tone got stern and loud enough that a few onlookers backed away from him.

"I'm serious about this! Listen." Now Czoltan pleaded with Galen. "I'm one of the ones listed in the warrant! I'm not dead!"

Sadly, the only person to whom this statement could possibly have made sense was entirely focused on the woman he clearly loved. Ears back, tail curled down, it wasn't even clear that he'd heard Czoltan. He kept opening his paws and closing them into fists, as though he wanted to punch the heart attack and then realized the futility of that action every few seconds. Following his gaze, I focused on Desiree.

She lay on the ground staring up into the face of the fox paramedic, but probably she wasn't even focusing on the russet muzzle. I couldn't see her pupils from Sergei's viewpoint. Her breaths came shallow and her limbs kept twitching despite the paramedics' restraint.

Should I appear? Sergei asked.

I thought about it. He would certainly disrupt the crowd, but I didn't think he'd be a more credible source than Czoltan. Ideally we'd want the other warrant officer to show up, but without Czoltan I had no way of knowing when that would be, and Czoltan wasn't checking his phone; he was struggling with the wolf paramedic and continuing to argue. One of the onlookers, a weretiger, had taken Czoltan's other arm and was trying to convince the paramedic that he could control this crazed biter.

No, I told Sergei, and stepped out from the shadow of the apartment. *I've got to do it.*

Jae—

If Galen looks like he's going to shoot me, appear in front of him again. But right now I don't know how long she's got, and I don't know how long the bite takes to be effective. It might already be too late.

I took out my military ID as I walked down the block. Sergei stayed at the scene but his voice got sharper. *I do not like this idea. You risk your life to save her? The wife of the man who tried to kill you?*

Not her fault, I said. *And I think he's really trying to kill her. Galen's the one who doesn't want to lose her. Look at him.*

There was a moment of silence. Then: *I will protect you as best I can,* he said.

I know you will, I told him.

Even with Sergei to back me up, I couldn't believe I was walking toward the guy with the gun who wanted to shoot me. But he was hurting, and that pain drew me to him with a pull I couldn't ignore, not when there was a chance I could still help.

After all, that's why I became a private eye in the first place: to help people. Sure, I'd gotten away from that in the past couple years, largely because the people I tried to help often didn't want my help or didn't deserve it.

Here, now, in front of me, was someone I could help—two people I could help—and I thought there was at least a reasonable chance that Galen wouldn't pull his gun and shoot me in the middle of a crowd of people. I was well aware that I thought this despite whatever he and his companion had been about to do at the plaza.

At the corner, I hesitated. Someone—a werewolf—crossing the street toward me stopped, noticing the crowd, and then jostled me in her hurry to see what was happening. I saw a chance and walked quickly behind her, keeping her between me and Galen so that if he happened to glance up, he wouldn't see me.

Czoltan saw me, though, and stopped his struggling to stare at me, trying to catch my eye, I was sure, so he could tell me to go back. I hated making him worry like that. Hell, I hated making Sergei and myself worry, for that matter, but I was breaking out in a sweat and the roaring in my ears wasn't going away.

When we got to the crowd, I crouched down and pushed through to get to the side of the huli jing. "Excuse me," I said, and held out my military ID. "I served in Kosovo. I've seen this before."

"Sir," she said, keeping her focus on Desiree, but a glance at my ID stopped her rote answer before it got any further. "You've seen this? You're sure?"

"Her husband served with me in Kosovo," I said. "I think he poisoned her. The convulsions are the key. You don't get those with a heart attack."

She searched my eyes and I knew that had hit home. "Well shit. What's the treatment?"

I sighed. "The bioweapon speeds up her metabolism until she dies. You've got her on blood thinners?"

"Yes."

"That'll help for a bit, but her heart's going to keep racing."

Now the fox sat back on her heels. "It doesn't feel like a standard heart attack," she admitted. "So what's the treatment? Is there one?"

"Hey!"

That was Galen's voice. He'd noticed me and drawn his gun. "That guy's a dangerous criminal!" he yelled.

Czoltan, bless him, shifted his struggles from the wolf paramedic to grabbing at Galen's arm so he couldn't get his gun up. "I'm alive!" he yelled. Galen stared at him. "I'm Czoltan Osmani. My name's on that warrant," Czoltan said. "It says I'm dead."

"What?" The other wolf looked dazed, but at least he let Czoltan restrain his gun arm.

"There's a false warrant," I emphasized those words, "out on me. It says I killed people including that guy." I pointed at Czoltan. "I'm trying to save your girlfriend's life, and I need your help. After that—you can arrest me if you want."

It took a few seconds for those words to sink in, but when Galen turned to look at Czoltan and saw his determination, he holstered his gun. "All right," he said, challenging me. "What do we do, then?"

"You've got to bite her," I told him. "Changing her metabolism is the only thing that will stop the poison. If it's not already too late."

The huli jing gave me a sharp look. "That's illegal," she said.

"Super illegal," the wolf paramedic added.

"It's permitted in exigent circumstances," I said.

The fox looked down at Desiree and back up at me. "We're the ones who have to make that decision. It's for if someone's bleeding out or something."

"Yeah, how do we know this bioweapon is even real?"

"I know it's a leap to trust someone you've never met—"

"What if you poisoned her?" This was Galen, still glaring at me, his paw near enough to his gun to make him feel confident.

"Then I wouldn't be trying to save her." I restrained myself from adding, "idiot," partly because I wanted to keep things civil and also because of the gun just below his twitchy fingers.

The huli jing looked up at her partner. "I don't know what else to do here."

"I don't either, but biting is serious." The wolf rubbed her whiskers. "Let's call it in. Maybe Chaz has some experience with this."

Czoltan had gotten the wolfsbane out and had the small tin close to Galen, but Galen watched the wolf paramedic. As she headed for the small emergency vehicle (like a small flatbed truck, basically two seats and a stretcher on wheels), Galen set his ears back and shifted his focus to me. "How long does she have?" he demanded, nostrils flaring.

"I don't know. And I don't know at what point the bite will still be effective."

Those words were true, but also I knew what effect they would have. Galen snarled and grabbed the tin from Czoltan. Startled, Czoltan froze before swiping at Galen, but by that time the warrant officer had already taken the drug into his mouth and started chewing.

"Hey!" The huli jing tried to keep her eyes and paws on Desiree and also stop Galen from getting near her patient. She succeeded in only the first part; Galen started toward Desiree's head and then swerved to her legs, bare and gleaming with sweat.

As he knelt next to her, the wolf called out from the vehicle, phone in her paw, "Sir! Hey, sir!"

The huli jing started to get up, and as I was close, I stepped over to her. "I don't think you should interfere," I said.

"This is an irreversible—"

Galen had already lowered his muzzle to Desiree's leg, chewing the wolfsbane. Many of the spectators had their phones out and were filming this. "She'll die if he doesn't," I said, hopefully loudly enough for twenty microphones to pick it up.

The fox paramedic started toward Galen anyway, but I'd delayed her enough that she didn't get there before he sank his teeth into Desiree's thigh.

I'd seen werewolves bite humans with the intent to change them, but only a handful of times, and most of those were under stress or aggressive. Galen's bite had a very different intensity to it. He closed his eyes, put a paw gently on her leg as his teeth closed and broke the skin, and then, holding her leg in his jaw, lifted his other paw and placed it on her stomach. If you ignored the trickles of blood that ran down past his teeth, he might have been embracing her. Or preparing to move his muzzle somewhere more pleasant.

He breathed evenly, and when the huli jing reached him and tried to pull him away, he resisted passively, the way a child might go limp to prevent a parent from picking him up. The fox tried to get her fingers in to pry his jaw away, but he held on tight, not even fending her off with his paws. Maybe he didn't want to break contact with Desiree.

It was a touching scene, and the crowd sensed it as well, going still (though they kept filming). After a tense twenty seconds or so, Galen released her leg and looked up at the crowd. His eyes settled on me. "I...don't know how long..."

The huli jing walked over to the kit on the ground by Desiree's head and took out a bandage and a spray. "It's done now," she said, coming back and pushing Galen away. She knelt and sprayed the wound.

"Hey." Galen started toward her and then stopped and swayed. The wolfsbane must have been kicking in hard. "You —you're not un—undoing it."

"You can't. I'm disinfecting the wound." She put the spray down and then wrapped the bandage quickly and tightly over the bite. "And Penny—my partner—is going to have to call that in."

"Already doing it," the wolf said.

"That's fine." He looked at me again and gave a goofy wolfsbane-drunk smile. "I saved her life." He swayed and pointed at himself. "*I* saved her life."

"You did," I told him.

The huli jing looked between us. "One of you two wouldn't by chance be her emergency contact, would you?"

"Ah, no," I said. "That'd be—"

Galen's eyes widened. "Oh, shit," he said. "Her husband."

The paramedic wolf, still holding her phone up to her ear, lowered it and put her paw over the mic. "She's married?"

"The problem is," I said, "her husband is probably the one who poisoned her."

They loaded Desiree onto the electric stretcher and settled Galen into one of the seats after giving him a sedative. Penny— the wolf—drove the two of them away.

The huli jing dispersed the spectators and then asked me to

come with her back to the hospital in a way that wasn't really asking but was phrased that way for politeness. While she was making a phone call to make sure there was a police presence at the hospital, I asked Sergei to follow them and make sure that the paramedics, if they called Richard, only told him that she'd fallen ill. He'd think that was according to his plan.

Not being able to see me talking to Sergei, a couple people in the crowd came up and gave me their contact information in case I needed their recordings for some reason. One was genuinely concerned about me; I think the rest just wanted to be part of an exciting drama. I managed to navigate dual conversations well enough to get Sergei going while still being polite to the helpful onlookers.

Right as the last one finished up, a wolf in a blue collared shirt and mud-brown slacks came walking up and pushed his way between me and the huli jing. "This man," he proclaimed, pointing at me, "has been falsely accused."

"We got there," I said. "It's cool. But thanks."

Czoltan, who'd been lurking near me, came forward. "Val, thanks," he said. "We handled it, though."

Val looked around, panting. "Where's the woman?" He turned on Czoltan. "You said a woman was in danger."

"We handled it," Czoltan repeated.

"I really appreciate you coming anyway," I said.

Val folded his arms. "If you could've handled it, why did I leave my job and run all the way here?"

"Because you're a nice guy?" Czoltan tried a smile.

Val rolled his eyes. "Glad everything worked out," he said stiffly, and turned on his heel and left.

The paramedic fox watched him go. "What a dick," she said. "You were trusting your life to him?"

"He would've come through," I said with more certainty than I felt.

"I only know him a little bit," Czoltan said.

The huli jing shook her head. "Come on," she said. "Let's go to the hospital. You coming too?"

Czoltan looked to me for confirmation. "Sure," I said. "If you don't mind."

"I don't mind." He stepped up beside me.

I knew I needed to say something more, but it was a struggle. After a mental kick in the butt, I said, "I'll feel better if you're there."

"Good," he said, and his tail wagged in a way that tugged at my heart.

At the hospital, Officer Mara Pulaski, an actual werewolf police officer rather than a warrant officer, took me into custody with an uncertain apology. "We have to do this until we can verify that the warrant is false," she said.

"The warrant says I'm dead," Czoltan protested. "Can't you verify that?"

"There could be another wolf with your name," Pulaski said. "There's no picture on the warrant, but there might be in the original filing."

"It's fine," I told Czoltan. "I need to figure out what to do next anyway."

I didn't want to say in front of an officer that I was going to apprehend Richard, because she would definitely tell me that that was not my job. Maybe it wasn't. But he'd tried to have me killed, or at least had used me as a prop in his stage play to get his wife killed. And besides, if anyone was going to bring in my dead old Army captain, it ought to be me.

CHAPTER 8
BECOME THE HUNTER

The police took me from the hospital out of Wolftown and to the local station, where they put me in a jail cell with a blanket and an apology. At least they let Czoltan stay outside the cell and talk to me while they went about clearing up the warrant, and they were nice enough to let me plug my phone in—outside the cell. I called my lawyer and caught him up on the situation and then passed him off to the officer in charge.

Jo finally texted me back on the drive, which I only knew because the arresting officer who'd taken my phone told me so. I told him he could text back on my behalf telling her what was going on, but he just grunted and put the phone away. At the station, I asked if I or someone could text her so she wouldn't worry, seeing as how I'd told her I was in danger of my life, and the desk sergeant allowed me to text back, under her supervision.

So I told Jo what had happened and got the name of the local officer investigating the warrant to pass along to her.

Hopefully the two of them working together could clear things up pretty quickly.

That left me sitting in a jail cell with a werewolf on the other side of the bars. The police had taken my personal effects as standard procedure, including my ring, which meant that Sergei would have to manifest for us to talk. He wasn't doing that, and I didn't want to talk about trapping a ghost out loud anyway, not here.

Czoltan wanted to talk about anything but that, including whether Desiree would be okay (she'd still been unconscious when she got to the hospital), how long it would take the police to clear up the warrant, and of course: "Will I see you again after today?"

The image of Galen bending down to bite Desiree's leg, the love and tenderness there, stuck in my mind. Was that me, could it be me? It felt beyond me for reasons I couldn't pin down. "My situation," I said, and then stopped myself.

"I know, I know." Czoltan reached over to the desk he was sitting beside where a manila envelope rested. He slid a claw under the flap and worked it open.

I sat up straighter. That was the envelope with my personal effects. "Hey," I said.

He fished inside and came out with my ghost-binding ring. "If I put this on," he said, "can I talk to Sergei?"

"No, and you shouldn't put it on."

His ears perked up. "He's talking to me."

I leaned back against the wall of the cell. "Of course he is. Tell him to manifest so I can talk to him too."

"He says no." Czoltan raised his eyebrows. "He says he can't believe you let yourself get arrested. He says you could've gotten away while they were preoccupied with Desiree." He grinned as he conveyed that message.

"Of course we could have, and then we'd have gotten arrested leaving Wolftown or something."

He rolled his eyes and put the ring back in the envelope. "He says you could've stayed at my place. So nice of him to offer my hospitality."

"He likes you."

"Nice to know one of you does."

I exhaled. "I like you, too. Can I try to figure out how I'm going to deal with Richard?"

His eyes slid to the envelope. "Do you need to talk to Sergei?"

"There's cameras all over, maybe mics too. Don't give me anything or you'll get in trouble whether or not I'm cleared."

"Whether or not?" His ears perked.

I shook my head. "I will be, I hope, but as long as that fake warrant's up, I'm not a hundred percent that it's going to be cleared up easily. I have faith in Jo, though."

He nodded and leaned on the desk, tail swishing. I admired that he'd stayed in wolf form even outside of Wolftown; he could easily have shifted to human. Some extras considered it polite to do so; some considered it conforming to outside expectations. I thought that Czoltan just hadn't considered changing because this was who he was, and that was part of what I loved about him.

"Anyway," I went on, "the thing with Richard is tricky because ideally I'd want something like..." I gestured toward the envelope where he'd placed the ring. "I think I could do it. I don't think Sergei would be a problem."

He caught on to my reluctance to say the word "ghost" very quickly. "I thought you'd been with him four years."

"Sure, but I've just been with him. There are people who've had dozens and they have a lot more experience."

"So why not call one of them?"

"No time. I'd rather get over there before he realizes his plan didn't work, and that means...ideally by the end of the day."

"Would he even let you in? Doesn't he expect you to be dead?"

"If I spin the right story..." I worked through it in my head. *Desiree and that warrant officer she's cheating on you with shot at me, chased me through the streets, and then seemed to give up, I don't know why.* It might work.

He nodded. "I can take care of Sergei while you're doing it. If that would help."

"I'm sure he'd enjoy talking to you. I don't think there's much you can do if there's a problem, though."

"Oh." He lay his ears back and looked at the envelope.

"It's fine," I told him. "Sergei's polite. He doesn't respect boundaries, but he's polite. Usually. And if something happened, he'd come after me, not you. Or he'd just go."

"I'm not that worried." But his ears remained half-down and his fingers tapped quickly on the desk.

I touched the bars that separated us. "If you'd do that, then that'd make things at least a little easier."

"That's what I like to do," he said. "Make things easier."

I sighed. "I live in Chicago now."

"It's fine, Jae." He turned away. "You don't have to make excuses."

"What I was going to say was...I live in Chicago now, but I could maybe get up here now and then."

His ears came up. "'Now and then'? You think that's what I'm after?"

"Okay, well, what do you suggest? What do you want?" I stood and walked to the bars. "You want me to uproot my job and move here?"

"I want you not to have left," he said in a low voice.

While I understood that and part of me wished I hadn't left either, I also had a pretty successful practice in Chicago. I had a few friends, if not a lot, and I had a routine, a healthy theatre habit, and a whole vocabulary for complaining about the weather. It was comfortable and settled in a way that Detroit maybe could have been one day, but never quite had been, in part because I was always worried about my relationship. Not Czoltan himself, but losing him if my family didn't approve, if something happened.

Now? My family was still an issue. Why would I start something just to see how long it could last before my mom found out about it? I wasn't going to cut ties with my family and Czoltan wasn't going to become human, so where could this go?

Then why did you go on that date with Alan?

I actually told Sergei to shut up before realizing that the voice was in my own head.

"Yeah," I told Czoltan, "but I did. So what now?"

"I don't know! Maybe we should figure that out—"

The door behind him opened to admit the desk sergeant who'd helped me. "All right, all right," she said, waving a piece of paper. "Mr. Kim, it looks like the name of the submitting officer on this document was forged. Your friend Jo helped us clear it up and we verified that at least four of the five people listed as victims are still alive."

"So I'm free to go?"

She stopped at the table and dropped the paper onto it. "There's the matter of Ms. Desiree Collison. The hospital hasn't verified the presence of a bioweapon in her system. They've done a blood panel, but it'll be a few hours before that comes back. She's comfortable—she's going to pull through. So you're either a felon for turning her, or a hero for saving her life."

"Galen saved her life," I said. "I just told him how."

"Right." She seemed to be trying not to look amused. "By law, you'd be responsible primarily, with him as an accomplice, but based on the phone calls I've had with the Chicago PD about you, I'm going to go out on a limb and say that at least you believed what you were saying. Also got a call in to the DOD about K-118, but that could be months coming back. So I'm going to release you on your recognizance, but don't leave Detroit for a day or two until we get this sorted out. Fair?"

"Yes, of course." I stood back from the bars.

She came forward and unlocked the cell. "Can you stay out of trouble for twenty-four hours?"

"Absolutely," I lied.

The first thing I did was put on Sergei's ring and ask if the bear was all right.

Of course I am all right, he huffed. *I sit in darkness and remember the names of the dead who were my friends. How are you?*

Similar, I said. *Though less depressing.*

Is not depressing. Is duty. When I no longer remember, they are gone. I am the last—

I know, I know. I'm sorry about getting arrested.

Do not do it again. He punctuated that with a short laugh.

Once we walked out onto the sidewalk into the mass of non-extra humanity, Czoltan got the same kind of weird looks that I'd gotten in Wolftown, only more so, and he noticed them right away. His ears went flat self-consciously and then they slid down the side of his head and shed their fur as he shifted into a shirtless human, which was still notable, if less so. His human form was less familiar to me but even with his short dark hair and sharp nose and chin, I would've recognized the hazel eyes and the smile. He looked skinnier, probably because of the loss of all that fur, and less sure of himself.

"You don't have a spare shirt on you, do you?" he asked as we made our way down the steps of the station.

"We can get one if you want. I'd rather work out how we're going to bind Richard."

"I guess it's not that chilly out." He crossed his arms and rubbed them.

"Or you could just be a wolf again." I checked our location. I'd parked way over by the entrance to Wolftown, so I called a rideshare.

"People will stare."

"They're staring now."

He shrugged and glanced around. "Yeah, but now they're staring like 'who's the white trash guy,' and this is Detroit so it's not even that bad."

"You don't have enough tattoos to be a white trash guy from Detroit," I told him. "Especially hanging out in front of a police station."

He squinted. "How would you even know?"

"I go to the movies."

He rolled his eyes after a moment of hesitation in which I guessed he was trying to flick his ears or do something with the wolf ears he didn't have at the moment. "So how do you bind a ghost? What's involved?"

"Well...there's a bit of magic. I have the spell on my phone, just in case."

Ha.

"The ghost has to stick around long enough to be bound, but that's usually not a problem because they're often tied to a place. If they've been unbound long enough, they're kind of unmoored from reality so they won't run away anyway. They might throw something at you if they can do that."

Czoltan looked around warily. "Don't worry," I said. "Sergei won't throw anything at you."

Not out here in public.

"Can he?"

"I guess if he got really worked up enough. It takes experience, and Richard's got to be relatively recent, so I wouldn't worry too much about him."

"What am I going to have to do?" Czoltan asked.

"Not much, hopefully. Maybe keep an eye on Sergei. Speaking of..." I took out my phone and checked Google for magic shops. "There's only one magic shop in the whole Detroit area?" The rideshare pulled up. "All right, this is going to take a bit longer than I'd hoped."

We couldn't talk about ghosts in the rideshare, even though our driver was a very nice older woman who guessed right away that Czoltan was a werewolf. "I see 'em all the time," she said. "Nice people. Friend of mine married one. They live over on Larchmont, Jake and Marisa Lockwood. You know 'em?"

"No," Czoltan said politely while I retreated into my phone, checking the magic shop's website to make sure they had ghost-binding things.

Once we were in my car, I gave Czoltan my phone to direct me. "Up here, turn right," he said. "So just the spell and the binding, that's all?"

"Well...you can't just bind a ghost. I guess some people can, but they're good storytellers. The idea is that you have to know something about the ghost. There are people who specialize in talking to ghosts and getting their stories, and those people usually become ghost hunters. I can't imagine listening to a bunch of ghosts and figuring out what they're raving about, but there's good money in it if you can do it."

"Like being a therapist," Czoltan said.

"For violently disturbed people."

"They need therapists too."

"I suppose. At any rate, the ghost hunter tries to figure out what's keeping the ghost here, and then if you want to bind it, you have to tell it a story."

He squinted over from the passenger seat. "Like a bedtime story?"

You have never told me a bedtime story.

"No." I stared ahead. "You have to tell the ghost a story about your own life. Something that they can relate to. They've got to see that you understand at least some part of them. Then the spell has something to latch on to, and they'll submit to the binding."

"Oh, wow." He paused. "I don't know a lot about ghosts."

"Most people don't. I mean, they know that they exist, but they don't bother to find out anything more about them."

"Why did you get interested in them?"

"Oh, it was a long time ago..." I thought back. "I think it was something the VA recommended as part of our therapy. When I was looking for a partner for my PI work, it seemed logical to look for a ghost. I mean, they can go anywhere, spy on people—I'm far from the only PI to have one."

"Why doesn't everyone?"

"Well...for one thing, they're not allowed everywhere. There's restrictions."

Not so many.

"And a lot of people aren't comfortable with ghosts. But really I think the reason is that they bond so closely to you that it's really hard to have any privacy."

Czoltan looked at me again. "Left up here, then right at the next light."

I followed his instructions. "But I don't mind. Sergei's good company and even if he is a pain sometimes and watches me on dates, I know I can rely on him."

"You can rely on him because he has to obey you."

He's smart, this one.

"That's not what I mean. I mean, it is sort of, but—I know PIs who tried to work with another person as their partner. I only know one partnership like that that's lasted four years. Anyway, it's not like Sergei doesn't get something out of it. He gets to be sane."

Sane is, how do you say it, overrated.

"And," I added, "he makes pretty good jokes."

"All right." Czoltan pointed. "Turn right at that light and it should be a couple blocks down on the right."

We were in a high-end suburb of Detroit; the corner I turned on had a large Nordstrom's, and we drove past a bunch of other high fashion stores. The magic shop sat between a Palomino's restaurant and a Hilton hotel and was called, "Beyond the Pale."

"So," Czoltan said as we parked on the roof of the exorbitant parking structure across the street, "what story did you tell Sergei?"

I paused long enough for Sergei to chuckle into my head and then said, "That's, uh, kinda personal."

"Okay, sure." Here in a ritzier area, Czoltan's shirtlessness stood out, and as we stood at the parking garage elevator, he crossed his arms over his chest again. "Hey, what if they have a 'no shirt' rule?"

"Change to wolf," I said. "Go ahead and do it now if you want."

"In this area?"

165

A well-dressed couple walked toward us from their car, both deep in their phones. "I bet it'll get fewer stares than being a shirtless human. Anyway, nobody's going to come at you with silver here. Worst that'll happen is they'll call the police and you'll be politely asked to leave, and we'll be done by the time that happens."

He looked dubious, glanced over at the couple, and rubbed his arms again. "If this is anything like the same kind of neighborhood in Chicago, you'll be fine," I said. "Trust me."

That got me a raised eyebrow, but he stepped around the corner and re-emerged as wolf-Czoltan, tail curled down along his hip. I gave him a big smile and then turned back to see the couple's reaction.

The woman looked up from her phone, stopped, and then put on that upper class "nothing's wrong" face and elbowed the man. He looked up at her first, and then forward. And then they both noticed me watching them. "Oh," she said, "is he with you?"

I put my arm around him. "Yeah," I said, "he's with me."

"That's so marvelous," she said. "You know, a werewolf works with our son. She seems very nice."

"Yes, some of us are," Czoltan said.

We rode down with them in the elevator and they couldn't stop staring at him the whole time, while he stared straight ahead. We let them get out first and walked slowly enough that they pulled away from us. Czoltan didn't say anything, but strode with more confidence out into the street.

"So is there any danger in this?" he asked quietly while we were waiting at the light to cross the street.

I didn't say anything right away. After a moment, he went on. "Cause I feel like a lot more people would have bound ghosts if there weren't some kind of danger to it."

"Nothing's a hundred percent safe," I said. The light changed and I strode out into the street.

He hurried after me. "Okay, what could happen? Could Richard kill you?"

"Sure. He's got stuff in that house. There might be security measures. I don't think he could lift a gun to fire, but there might be other stuff." He'd gotten Desiree exposed to K-118, for one thing.

Czoltan kept scanning the crowd for people staring at him. There were a few, but nobody seemed particularly upset. "So what are you most worried about?"

You should tell him, Sergei said.

I know. But it took me a few more steps before I could formulate the words. "The binding spell exposes you to the ghost, and there's a chance that if you're not forceful enough with your story, the ghost could tell you its story, and then..."

"Then what?" he demanded when I didn't finish. "The ghost can possess you?"

"Maybe. Or you can get lost in the ghost's story and lose your grip on reality."

He lay his ears back. "Like...permanently?"

"I haven't looked up the statistics, but five years ago they had about a thirty percent success rate in bringing back guys. Out of like a thousand ghost bindings, that happened twenty or so times, so it's a small chance. Among people who took the ghost training." I paused. "Maybe it happened thirty times and it was a twenty percent success rate. Something like that, anyway."

His ears didn't come up, and his tail curled down. "I don't like it."

"I don't like it either, but remember, I've done this before. We had supervision last time, but I have an idea of what to expect."

167

Czoltan stayed quiet all the way over to "Beyond the Pale," where I had to show my ID and the credential from the ghost training I'd received (I keep all my important documents in a folder on my phone). The clerk, a middle-aged woman who kept saying, "I have to make sure you're not dabblers," even after I'd shown her my training certificate, finally brought out a small tray from a locked cabinet.

"I've only got these three anchors in the store," she said. "I can order another one if you don't like any of these."

The items we had to choose from were a tarnished silver cross, a round medallion with a five-pointed star embossed on it, and a copper ring. I didn't want something as permanent as a ring, and Richard wasn't religious enough for the cross, so I picked the medallion. "This'll be fine."

"Do you know what ghost you're going to bind? Sometimes the choice of object matters."

"I do. This one will be fine."

It cost fifteen hundred dollars, which was half again what I'd expected, and seemed like a lot to spend on a ghost I wasn't even going to keep. Maybe the police would reimburse me for it. I handed over my credit card and took the medallion.

"Happy hunting," the clerk said as she handed my card back. She smiled at Czoltan as well.

"See?" I said, clutching the paper bag in one hand as I held the door for the wolf. "She didn't even blink."

"She runs a magic shop," Czoltan said. "Of course she didn't. Hey, is there anything I can do? Like you said you had supervision last time. Can I do that? Supervise?"

I stood at the corner and swung the bag, then realized what I was doing and shoved it into my pocket to keep it safe. "I want you to be around, sure. I'm not sure there's any danger to you, but I can't have Sergei on while I do this, so if you could take care of him, that'd help."

He does not need to mind me.

I know. I'm trying to give him something to do so he feels useful. Ahh.

"Sure, I can do that." He glanced at my ring. "Will he talk to me again?"

"If he wants to." The reality of having the binding token nudged me to get the binding spell up on my phone so I could study it.

Czoltan peered over my shoulder. "That's the spell?"

"Uh huh."

"You just have to say those words?"

"With the right intonations. We had to practice them for two weeks before we got them right." I didn't want to hide anything from him, but his staring also made me uneasy, so I put the phone away. "Sorry, I'm not supposed to show them to anyone who hasn't gone through the course."

"Oh yeah." He took a step away from me and ducked his head. "Sorry."

We got back to the car and strapped in, Czoltan grumbling as the seatbelt pinched his fur. "These things aren't made for wolves," he complained.

I didn't respond, preoccupied by navigating the parking garage and also by the awareness that this was it. The next stop was going to be Richard's house and then I was going to have to do this thing.

Maybe I should call the police after all, I mused to Sergei. *This is all speculation on my part.*

If he is a ghost, Sergei replied, *then you must report him, and if you can bind him then you are legally allowed to do so.*

That's true.

Ghosts have no rights, he added mournfully. *But you have not proven that he is ghost. Only suspected. He might be crazy person who wanted to kill wife.*

We don't say 'crazy,' I told Sergei, but that was a possibility I hadn't considered in a while. I could've just spent fifteen hundred dollars for nothing. Also, if Richard wasn't a ghost, then he could wield a knife or a gun pretty easily. I didn't want to bring a gun into his house, and my bulletproof vest was back in Chicago where idiot me had left it, thinking this was going to be a routine tail.

So...should I just call the police? I asked Sergei.

That would be prudent course, he replied as though he'd been thinking about the same thing.

My phone told me we were twenty minutes away. *You didn't say 'yes.'*

You have not told me why you have not.

Yeah, I'm trying to figure that out.

"Are you talking to Sergei?" Czoltan asked.

"Yeah. Sorry."

"It's okay. You just went all quiet." He stared ahead of us at the road. "I was wondering why you didn't tell the police the truth. Couldn't they help you with this?"

I nodded. "They could."

"But?"

"But. Yeah." I turned onto the expressway. "Part of it is that I'm an investigator, you know? I want to find out answers. If the cops lock up Richard, I might never know what happened —how he died, if he died, and what went on with Desiree."

"Wait," Czoltan said. "'If' he died? You're not sure he's a ghost?"

My ears warmed. "I haven't proven it. He could be a germaphobe who really is afraid of ghosts and doesn't like strong-smelling cleansers. But. Too much points in the other direction. He's acting very erratically, he won't let people in the same room with him, and he kept Sergei outside the house. I'd say I'm 95 percent—no, 98 percent sure."

The wolf settled back into his seat. "All right."

"But back to your question: I think part of it too is that Richard and I were close. He looked out for me on a lot of missions. We went through hell together. If the cops catch him, they'll just banish him. And I don't want to put him through whatever that is. I owe him that much."

Do you really? Sergei asked. *You had not spoken to him in years. And he tried to kill you.*

"Do you, though?" Czoltan asked at the same time.

"Neither of you knew me when I was friends with Richard, not early on," I said. "He was my commanding officer for years, but he was my friend, too. We went through that shitty war together, protected each other. Sure, we argued, but I knew I could count on him and he could count on me."

Both of them stayed silent. "I know it's dangerous, but we lived through dangerous times together. He risked his reputation by keeping my secret with you," I told Czoltan. "So...I think I have to do this. I think about turning it over to the police and I know it makes sense but it doesn't feel right."

Sergei stayed quiet and Czoltan just said, "Huh."

I didn't know what else to say. We were a mile from the exit that would bring us closer to Richard, and then I was pulling off the expressway. "What does Sergei say?" Czoltan asked.

"He hasn't said anything yet."

I respect loyalty to fellow warrior. I jumped in front of axe for my friend once. Death through such honor will bring you endless joy in the world beyond.

"Okay," I said, "that's a very Russian answer. He says if I die, it'll be worth it because I'm acting with honor."

"I don't want you to die," Czoltan said. "But I can't really argue with your feelings. If that's how you feel, then you should do it. Sergei and I will help however we can."

"Really?"

TIM SUSMAN

Yes.

"Yeah. Loyalty matters, you know. And you said it's not all that dangerous. If you feel good about doing this, then...yeah, let's do it. I'd hate for you to be regretting—" He stopped. "That was going to become snarky, and I didn't mean it that way. I just mean that he's a friend, and if you can help him out, you should do it."

Especially if it means they will not banish him.

CHAPTER 9
THE STORY

At Richard's house, I sat in the car for several minutes before getting out, enough that Czoltan asked if I was up for this.

"I'll be fine," I said. "It's just, you know, hard to go bind your dead friend into a necklace."

You did not have such problem with me.

I didn't know you.

So this should be easy for you.

"You have to do it, though. He's dangerous. He might try to kill his wife again."

"I know, I know." I sighed and took off Sergei's ring. "Here. Take care of him."

"I will." He took the ring in two fingers. It wouldn't fit over his furry wolf digits, so he tucked it into his pants pocket. "I'll keep my fingers on it, I promise."

I got out and closed the door as he got out the other side. "So," he said, "should I wait at the car or what?" He had one paw stuck in his pocket, holding onto Sergei's ring. "I've never done anything like this before."

We'd spent the whole car ride over here debating whether to do this, but we'd barely talked about how. His earnestness helped relax me as I tried to figure out how to keep him safe and downplay my own danger. "If you want to support me, you should come in as well. He knows you, so it won't be suspicious. When I actually start the binding, it might be hard for you to tell what's happening. Sergei won't be able to see through you or me, so he might ask you to describe it for him. Make that as quiet and subtle as you can so you don't distract Richard. I'll need his attention."

Czoltan nodded. "I can do that. And—" He paused, listening in the way that people talking to a ghost do. "And if things go wrong?"

"You'll know. I'll give you a signal. I'll...I'll raise both arms over my head."

"And then what do I do?"

"Come take the necklace away from me and throw it away. Oh, without touching it. That's all. If I'm still non-responsive, call 911 and tell them you have a paranormal emergency."

"How do I take it away without touching it?"

I nodded to the glove compartment. "There's a cloth in there you can take."

He found it and followed me up to the door as I got myself into the right state of mind. I didn't have lines that I was trying to memorize; I just wanted to build up the story I was going to tell to get in, as well as the one that I was going to use to bind him. The first was a lie, and so required more work.

I rang the doorbell.

For minutes, nobody answered. I rang it again, and still nothing. I was about to ring for a third time when my phone buzzed. Richard had texted: *What are you doing here?*

You sent me to follow your wife, remember? I did. I've got the results.

He couldn't very well say that he was surprised to see me alive without revealing that he knew about the fake warrant. But I knew he was thinking it. Anytime I came back with results for a private client, they might be unsure they wanted to see them, but they always dithered aloud or sounded afraid. Richard sounded angry and suspicious. *What's the wolf doing here?*

I showed Czoltan the text and the answer as I typed it. *You remember Czoltan. We ran into each other in Wolftown and he wanted to catch up.*

"Hi." Czoltan leaned in and waved.

Another long pause. Richard was at this point certainly wondering whether his fake warrant had worked. In his place, I would wonder whether it had been tagged by the police as fake. Czoltan's presence, when he was one of the victims listed on the warrant, wasn't good news in that regard.

Why don't you tell me what you've found from out there?

I'd rather tell you face to face.

He didn't say anything, so I went on. *Police are coming and I want to talk to you before they arrive.*

After a moment, I added, *Please.*

For a moment I wasn't sure that would work. The police could be coming to arrest him, but also just to tell him that his wife was dead. Nothing I'd said indicated I knew he was a ghost.

The door lock clicked open. I pulled the door open, and Czoltan and I walked inside.

The house was just as I'd left it that morning, with the same faint smell of Desiree's perfume. Richard texted me to go to the study again, but instead I went to the master bedroom. The door was locked, as I expected, but not deadbolted, and there was a couple millimeter gap between the door and the frame, so it was easy enough to get a tool in and push back the latch.

"What are you doing?" Richard's voice came through the door. "Don't come in here. I told you, you're dirty, stay outside."

"You're not a germaphobe," I said.

"Sergeant Kim!" His voice carried enough of its old authority to make me pause for a second. "Step away from this door. That is an order."

"We're not in the Army anymore," I said. The lock gave way to my tools. I signaled to Czoltan to wait in the hallway and pushed the door open against a thick pile carpet. It took me a moment to set my phone to record, and then I slipped it into my shirt pocket, camera out, and walked in.

Desiree's perfume permeated this room more strongly; too strongly, in fact, for it to be simply the residue of her presence. I surveyed the room and noted that on top of the large vanity, a bottle lay unstoppered and on its side. I didn't spend much time thinking about that because my attention flew immediately to Richard, standing at the foot of the large king bed and looking daggers at me.

"How do you know I'm not a germaphobe?" he demanded. "Don't you know how dangerous it is to trigger someone's phobia?"

I'd lived with a ghost for four years. I knew Sergei was a ghost even when he was manifesting as solidly as Richard was now. Though he was standing on the carpet, the thick pile remained fluffy and upright under his weight, not squashed as it was under mine. "If you're a germaphobe," I said, "why is there dust on those chairs? Why doesn't it smell like cleaning products in here?"

He shifted his lack of weight—habits die hard for ghosts—

and pointed an accusing finger at me. "You're not allowed to tell someone that their phobia is invalid."

I reached into my pocket and took out the paper bag, and from it the necklace with the star. As Richard watched me, I put the necklace over my head. "I wouldn't tell you that if you were really a germaphobe," I said. "But you're a ghost. I'm so sorry. How did it happen?"

He gathered himself up. For a moment I thought he might throw something at me. I had the binding spell all ready to go, but it would be easier if I were sure about what was keeping him here, and I wanted him in a calm state of mind. After his first flash of anger, his shoulders slumped. "Heart attack," he said. "I was shoveling snow. Stupid. I knew—I knew it would kill me."

"I'm sorry," I said again. "But Desiree kept you here?"

"Of course she did." His voice got some force back in it. "Of course! I swore I'd never leave her, promised with all my heart, and then that same stupid fucking heart up and betrays me. You can't imagine how it feels."

"I know—"

"You can't imagine, Jae," he insisted. "The weight of it, like stones tied to my feet, like Marley's chains."

"So you decided to kill her. That way you'd never leave her."

He showed no surprise at my reveal. "Her mother's going into surgery on Tuesday and she's been calling every day. She promised to be there. If she dies, she'll be bound here the same as I was, by a promise she can no longer keep. We'll be together."

I wasn't sure that would work, but I could see the ghost logic. "And what about me? What did I do to you?"

"Sergeant Kim." His smile stretched in a horrible way. "You were a convenience. You had left my life. I thought perhaps you might also become a ghost because of your abandoned ex, and then we might have had some time together, but believe me when I say that I didn't care one way or the other." He walked slowly toward me. "You said you had news about Desiree? Has she passed?"

I took a step back to the threshold of the bedroom. Czoltan, in the hallway, perked his ears toward me, but I gave him a small shake of my head. "She's in critical condition," I said. "You used K-118, didn't you? There's still some of it around."

"I knew it would come in handy." He stopped a foot from my face. If I hadn't had so much experience with Sergei, it would be very strange to be so close to a person and feel no warmth, no breath from their mouth. "I hoped we might prosecute those bastards for using a bioweapon, but that never happened. I promise I didn't think I'd ever use it, but..." His smile stretched tight and harsh. "When you need an untraceable way to kill someone..."

"How did you even get it on her?"

"Asked her to get my old Army stuff out of the basement. Loosened the top on one of the canisters when she picked it up."

"Well, it worked," I said, and then realized that if it had worked, Desiree would be a ghost and would be here right now, so I added, "She's going to die."

"Ahh," he said, relaxing enough that I thought for a moment that he might just pass to the other side and I'd avoid all this trouble. But then he went on. "'Going' to die? She's not dead yet?"

His tone was calm, but I knew something was wrong. "Not yet."

"But she was chasing you four or five hours ago, terrified for her life." His face pressed closer to mine, so close that I could see all the little unrealities in it. The hairs of his stubble were clear when I looked right at them, but in my peripheral vision they flickered. His eyes swam with specks and changed color from blue to hazel to brown and back. "If she's not dead yet, then how do I know she'll die?"

I reached up to grab the necklace and I started the spell. Richard's words cut through. "Could it be because you let a wolf bite her?"

Finish the spell. Finish the spell. The words seemed to take forever.

"You think I would send you out and not follow you? Not wait outside Wolftown to make sure?" He snarled the words.

Why did you let me in, then? I wanted to ask, but I had to finish the spell.

"You've cursed me to be alone forever. And now I'm going to punish you."

I finished the spell. My fingers clenched around the necklace. "Richard," I said, "listen to me."

"No," he said, "you listen to me. I knew you were coming to bind me. I'm ready for you. And when your binding fails, I'm going to take over your body. And then we're going to go to the hospital and finish the job."

During the training to get my binding certification, the most unsettling thing we did was talk to a ghost. Ghost speech comes into your head strangely, like your own thoughts wandering off on a tangent, not like you're listening to headphones (which is what most of us expected). We don't have any practice distinguishing alien thoughts in our head because we've never had to do that, so it takes a while. We had ten sessions with a ghost introducing thoughts into our head while our instructor schooled us on the techniques necessary to partition those thoughts.

Once a ghost is bound, they're much better behaved; they can talk to you like they're whispering in your ear and they respect the boundaries you enforce. An unbound ghost you're trying to bind is nowhere near as well behaved. Their thoughts blend with yours, and if you're not trained, you can lose yourself easily, especially if the ghost has had a lot of practice invading minds.

Richard had not had a lot of practice, which I hoped would give me an advantage. Still, his aggression and the speed with which he attacked after I'd finished the spell caught me off guard. He might not have been practiced, but he had all the unchecked passion and fury of a desperate ghost.

Think of those sleepless nights you've had where your mind latches on to a problem and magnifies it and spins it up into something insoluble. Think of how lonely and desperate you feel in those times. Being a ghost, I'm told, is a lot like that, except there's no sleep to reset your mind; there's no waking life to give you perspective. Some ghosts hold onto their sanity a little longer; some lose their grip quickly.

Richard had gone quickly. As soon as the spell finished, a tempest of emotion and images roared into my mind. Through a window rose the hills of Kosovo, the same brown I remembered dotted with scraggly bushes that had somehow escaped being trampled, run over, or dug up. I smelled sweat and blood and terror mixed with gasoline and the bleach of army laundry. I held a woman in my arms, but it wasn't a Kosovan woman; it was Desiree. I stared down into her dark brown eyes and felt her love reaching out to me like a tangible thing, tendrils wrapping around my heart and holding me close to her.

Desperate, I tried to hold her close, but her body resisted

180

like sand, pouring around my arms and fingers even as bonds of love still shimmered between us. I looked around for help and saw that my companions on the bus all held someone as well, and the shimmering tendrils that linked me to Desiree rippled between each couple. Over the rumbling of the bus and the jolts of the uneven dirt road, my fellows moaned all around me, giving voice to my silent anguish.

Outside the bus, a figure approached, taller than the bus, as tall as a building. His black cloak billowed like smoke around him and his footsteps sounded with the dull thud of mortar shells. I couldn't see his face, but I didn't have to. The wave of air he drove before him chilled my blood, and even as he reached a hand down to the bus I knew what would happen.

His fingers, smoky and unreal, passed through the roof of our bus and through the first couple. As deliberately as a musician plucking strings, he touched each glowing filament that connected the couple, and with his touch the light faded and the tendril crumbled to dust. When all the connectors were gone, the dying person gave a long sigh and sank through the floor of the bus as their companion cried out and clutched at empty air.

I couldn't let go of my Desiree, my dearest, my light, because if she slipped away from me, the light around my heart would go out and I could not bear that. All I could hope was that the bus would reach its destination before she died. So I had to watch, powerless, as Death ripped apart couple after couple, until finally we were all that was left.

The hills outside had turned black, any trace of life vanished from them, and still the bus rumbled on through hazy, thick air. Death, keeping pace, reached into the bus and his cold finger touched one of the tendrils between me and Desiree.

(wait)

With his first touch, it felt as though he'd pressed his icy finger directly onto my chest. I screamed as the light died and I lost a piece of Desiree. Another tendril, then another, and even as I gathered her in my arms as best I could, the light in those eyes dimmed and with the last connection between us breaking, finally went out.

I pressed my face to the cold glass of the window. Death stopped, standing amid the barren hills, now holding a cloud of glowing spirits that flitted about as though encased in a glass prison I couldn't see. He'd taken them all and the bus now carried us farther and farther from them.

Cold ran through my body. I wanted to strike at Death, to charge him and beat him down, to take back what he'd stolen from me. Come on! I yelled to the other passengers. They roused, slowly at first and then with more excitement as I stomped my way to the front of the bus.

The driver, as blank a person as Death, sat hunched over the wheel. I wrenched him out of his seat and threw him to the floor. The others swarmed him, silencing his protests as I took his place.

With a great effort, I pulled the steering wheel around and around, and the bus, groaning, left the road to clatter and jolt over the blackened soil. The drive to chase down Death, to reunite what he'd torn apart, consumed me. When his immense form came into view through the windshield, I slammed my foot down on the accelerator and gripped the wheel so hard I thought my icy hands might break.

The bus no longer seemed material around me, but an extension of myself thundering over dead ground. The others behind me cheered me on, crying out "get him!" and "let's roll!" The memory of Desiree's love wrapped around my heart,

(wait)

the ache to get it back stoked by the encouragement of the

others. We were all on a mission together to save our loves and save ourselves, to right the horrible wrong that had been done on this bus. Sometimes it felt as though we were running together, a herd of angry horses stampeding; sometimes I felt myself part of the mechanism of the bus, the engine belching diesel smoke and the frame almost coming apart at every jolt of the worn tires.

A hand fell onto my shoulder or onto the steering wheel or maybe the ground became tarry and sticky. Our progress forward slowed even though I pressed forward.

"Wait."

"No!" I roared. "No waiting! We can fix this! I can fix this!"

"Wait," the voice said again.

Still I tried to press forward, toward—toward—I could no longer see through the hazy air, but Death was ahead of me, I knew he was, and even though the ground clung to my wheels to my boots to my feet I pushed on. Wait? Wait for what? For Desiree

(no)

to be lost forever?

"Richard."

The voice was my voice. The name was my name—no, the name wasn't my name. My name was—

"Jae," I croaked back. "Don't you see? Don't you understand?"

"I do," I answered. "I know how much it hurts."

"Then you know what I have to do."

"This isn't the only way."

"Yes it is!" I roared.

My passion gave my wheels purchase, cleared the air for a moment. Death loomed before me, the spirits of the lost still trapped in his grip. I gave voice to my rage and loss and leapt forward.

"Richard."

"You won't stop me!" I cried. I seized his neck and found it substantial, more substantial than Desiree had been. My hands squeezed as my feet churned forward.

"You've already lost," my voice said through the pressure of my hands.

I turned away and looked into the face of the person speaking and saw my own features, calm and composed, as though the constriction on his on my neck were perfectly normal. "I've won," I told him. "We're on our way and you're on board. There's no way to stop me now."

"You've lost," I said back. "Just look."

I'd taken my eyes off Death for a moment and now turned back and searched the landscape for that tall, unmistakable figure. Gone. Nothing lay before me but blackened land, tendrils of smoke rising from it and disappearing into the grey sky. Despair crested and broke, driving me forward into the empty landscape.

"Now," I said, "let me tell you a story."

The remains of Richard's immersive dream clung to me as I tried to build my story in response, which made things difficult because I'd intended to use our shared experiences, though not Breg-lumi specifically. He'd already painted his loss of Desiree in the most apocalyptic terms, when all I wanted to do was show him that we'd shared experiences.

I'd wanted to start in Wolftown, but as I built the story, the canvas walls of one of the tents at the Red Cross camp rose around us. Carbolic acid and bleach aromas wafted in on the chill breeze along with the dirt and forest smells of Kosovo and the salt tang of the sea not too far behind. Outside came noises of movement familiar to both our memories: men walking, casual conversation just outside the limits of our comprehension, humvees rumbling through occasionally.

I sat in a canvas chair across from Richard as I'd known him then, with fewer wrinkles and more hair, staring me down with the same guarded aggression he'd used to keep the war at bay. I fought to keep him separate; the merging of our identities in the dream had been difficult to undo and it kept flickering back into this story.

"You can't do this," he said before I could start. "I'm stronger than you are. I've had weeks to practice, weeks to study, and I'm the stronger man anyway."

"We'll see." I held out my hand and willed a glass of scotch to appear in it. "Drink?"

He sneered at me and the glass disappeared. "We are only here because I'm allowing it."

I summoned the glass again and took a sip. "Keep believing that if it makes you feel better." The glass was inconsequential in the grand scheme of things, but I didn't like that he could get rid of it so easily. I needed to keep my focus sharp. "But you're going to hear me out. I know how it feels to lose Desiree."

"Ha." He leaned back in the chair. "Are you going to tell me about your father?"

"No." I gestured to the tent entrance, and Czoltan walked in.

Not the real one, of course; he was outside in the hallway watching to make sure nothing happened to me. This Czoltan came from my memory, though he'd been updated to look like the one waiting outside.

Richard took in the werewolf and then looked back at me. "Oh, ho," he said. "You're going to give me your breakup story finally? Go ahead, Jae. Lay it on me."

I took a breath and leaned back in my own chair. The reality wavered; the chair was there, but leaning back didn't bring me to a point where I might fall. "I didn't want to lose him," I told Richard, looking at my memory-generated ex-boyfriend. "I love—loved him. But my family never would have accepted a werewolf. It wasn't fair to him to draw it out any longer.

"It's not the same as losing someone to death, but here's what we have in common: the guilt. You feel guilty for abandoning your wife. I feel guilty for abandoning my boyfriend. But both of those happened because of the world around us. I can't change my family. You can't come back to life. But we have to do the best we can."

"I'm angry that Jae broke up with me," mind-Czoltan said, drawing Richard's attention. "I really thought things would work out."

I'd more or less scripted that stilted, awkward confessional, but as I was about to resume my own speech, Czoltan unexpectedly kept going. "What made me angriest was how he painted himself as the victim. He wouldn't even tell me the real reason, just said that things wouldn't work, made a bunch of flimsy excuses, and left."

"That sounds about right." Richard fixed me with a stare. "The same thing he did with the Army, the same thing he did with our friendship. He runs away rather than tackle things head on."

"Hey," I said. "Sometimes it's better to run away than to get caught in a fight."

"Or jump off a roof rather than talk your way out of a situation?"

"They were going to kill me! Sergei—" Sergei wasn't here. "I didn't have a choice."

"You always have a choice." Richard leaned forward. "That's what I did. I took the choice to stay, to reunite rather than allow the world to keep me apart from the person I love."

"That's not a choice! Ghosts aren't a rational decision."

"They're emotional. You should try being emotional sometime."

Czoltan, whom I was suspecting owed as much to Richard's mind as to mine, nodded emphatically. "He was always reserved. Even when he was breaking up with me, he didn't cry."

"I cried so much!" I yelled at him. "Just not in front of you!"

"Because God forbid you share any emotion."

"That's not fair." The tent shimmered around me; I exerted control and focus. "We shared a lot of emotion."

"When it was convenient for you. What about just now? When I yelled at you in my townhouse? What kind of emotion did you share then? Or did you just stand there and then walk downstairs?"

"Running away again," Richard put in. "You don't have to run away."

"I wasn't—I was giving him space." How much of this was Richard and how much was me? My chair wobbled under me and the tent shimmered again. Rents appeared in the canvas, showing only grey haze beyond. "I went back—"

"Because you had to," Czoltan said. "Not because you wanted to. Because you were hoping to avoid it."

"Because it was hard!" I stood, abandoning the decaying chair. "What point is there in going back when nothing's changed?"

"Hasn't it?" Richard stood and took a step toward me. "Hasn't it, really? Then why is he here with you in my house right now?"

"He's compassionate," I snapped. "He couldn't turn down someone who needed help, even if that someone broke his heart."

"That's how I know your whole story is bullshit." Richard stepped closer, a foot away from me, close enough that I

187

could smell his breath and after-shave. "You can go back. You did go back. But you're trying to stop me from going back. That's the difference between us. That's why this isn't working."

"No, it's not—"

Czoltan's hand fell on my shoulder. "Jae, are you all right?"

The pressure felt more real than the rest of my dream-story. Was Czoltan in the real world checking on me? Was I only imagining it? I was losing control.

When I looked away from Czoltan, Richard's eyes met mine, but they weren't the sky-blue eyes he'd had while alive. They were deep black pools, and I was falling into them.

"Jae."

I struggled to answer Czoltan. "I'm all right," I said, though I wasn't. I tried to push Richard away, but I couldn't look away from his eyes. The sounds around me faded into a background whine—

—no—

—the whine of jets approaching.

Familiar panic flooded me and long-dormant but never forgotten reactions kicked in. "We have to get to cover."

"No," Richard said, "we're gonna ride this one out."

"You're not thinking clearly." I couldn't move my feet.

He smiled. "I'm already dead is what I am. Don't worry. We're in your mind. What's the worst thing that could happen?"

The worst thing that could happen to me is you, I wanted to say, but part of me welcomed the idea that we could be torn up by strafing fire. (Who would attack a Red Cross camp? Never mind, this wasn't real.) Death wasn't all that bad, especially if you wanted to become a ghost. No more being weighed down by your body, no more headaches or muscle cramps or broken bones or diseases.

No more coffee or bibimbap, I argued. No more of the touch of a lover.

The whine drew closer. In the real world, we would have to be under shelter by now.

(What would happen if we died in the dream-story? My training had only covered that with the succinct, "We're not sure, so...don't.")

I switched tactics. Rather than fighting with Richard, I changed the tent we stood in. Canvas gave way to steel and concrete, the claustrophobic weight of a bunker around us. It should stand up to any strafing the Serbian air force could throw at it. We'd be safe...probably.

But Richard didn't seem worried, if he had indeed orchestrated this and it wasn't a trick of my own mind. "Putting up walls is just another way to run away," he said.

"Protecting your loved ones isn't running away."

"It's not taking action."

"What do you want me to do?" I gestured to the ceiling. "Punch the jets out of the sky?"

"You could have tried. It's your dream, isn't it?" He laughed. "Too late now, though."

"It's not—"

My words were blown away in a blast of gunfire.

I dropped to the ground and curled up, making the smallest possible target of myself. Bullets tore through the concrete around us, and though they might not have been real, the repeated concussions of gunfire growing into the roar of some crazed metal beast felt real to my ears; the small jolt of every impact became an earthquake to my body; the battle between the fear that this would last forever and the knowledge that it would be over in seconds consumed me.

The roar and the earthquake died away; the fear receded with the whine of the jets. I uncurled to the smell of smoke and dust and got to my knees in front of a pair of camo pants: Richard.

He reached down to help me up. Before he could turn his head to call my attention to the doorway, I was looking for Czoltan.

He lay across the threshold of the bunker. Red-stained holes marred his shirt, and midway down the right side of his chest, a gaping wound had been ripped open, revealing ugly maroon flesh with splashes of bright red blood streaming from it. His muzzle lay to the side and his eyes stared blankly back at me.

"No," I croaked. I ran hands down my shirt, wondering how I could be unharmed when Czoltan lay dead.

"You can't protect them forever." Richard's eyes blazed. "You can't be together in life forever. But you can be together in death."

"I'm not going to kill myself."

"Don't be an idiot." He scoffed at me. "You know what I'm talking about."

"I'm not going to kill him either."

"You'd lose him forever?" His smile tightened. "Ah, I forgot, you already did that."

"I didn't—" I struggled with this reality. Czoltan wasn't dead. He was standing a few feet from me, waiting for a sign he wasn't sure he'd be able to read.

"You did." Richard leaned in close. His breath stank of rot and blood. "You cut him out of your life. You didn't make any effort to get him back even though neither of you was dead."

"Stop—stop talking about him." I wrenched my gaze away from his corpse.

"You chose this story. You thought this would show what we have in common." Richard stepped back. "You didn't realize that you want him back as much as I want Desiree, that what we have in common is that need. That's why you're losing this fight. If you even want to call it a fight."

I pressed my hands to my head. I did want Czoltan back, but that wasn't why I'd picked his story. That wasn't what Richard and I had in common. He was right; there was the want, but there was something else. If want was all there was, the situation would have been easier.

When I looked at his body, I felt the pain I'd expected, but there was more: there was regret. I'd missed four years with him because of a decision I'd made, a decision motivated not by want, but by something darker and deeper.

"Together." His voice echoed in my head. "Together we'll go out and reunite with those we lost. You can have Czoltan again."

The temptation sank claws into me. I could have it, if—

—if I gave in to Richard, we would go to the hospital and I would commit a murder. I'd be arrested. I'd lose Czoltan.

"It doesn't have to go that way. She's a werewolf now. You know how to kill werewolves."

I couldn't help looking at Czoltan's corpse, but it was gone, not even bloodstains remaining on the ground. The bunker around us had lost detail: the walls were smooth grey rather than concrete blocks; the floor was the same featureless flat color, and the chairs I'd created were gone. Only Richard and I remained.

Czoltan was a werewolf. Ordinary bullets couldn't kill him, even if they tore open his chest like that. I clung to that little discrepancy. Those were the things that let me work my fingers into the cracks of the story and pull it apart, reimpose my will on it.

"He's not gone," I said steadily to Richard. "That's not what the story's about."

"Of course it is." But his eyes flickered.

"No. It's about fear. That's what we share."

I pushed away the bunker, the floor, all the trappings of the dream until Richard and I floated in darkness, just the two of us alone. "You're changing your story," he sneered. "A desperate move."

"We both saw Breg-lumi in the war. We saw so many people lose someone that we can't imagine anything but the end of our time with someone. We're so terrified of that ending that we'll do anything to stop it. We'll push someone away so that they don't get taken from us. Or we'll plan the murder of someone we love because we're terrified of losing her."

I said that last part deliberately, staring into his eyes. He glared right back. "You don't know what you're talking about. You haven't been with her and not with her at the same time until it drives you crazy."

"No," I said. "But I've felt the same fear you have." I reached my arms out to him. "I covered it up with a lot of excuses, but there are no excuses here. Can you see it? Can you feel it?"

He resisted, but I kept my arms outstretched. He lurched toward me, then stiffened and stood his ground one more time. "Everyone has fear," he said.

"Everyone has fear, but not like this. Not pounded into our lives over years, not so much a part of us that it rules how we look at relationships, that it keeps you from accepting your own death, for the love of God."

"I—"

There was a ripple in the world and then he shuddered and deflated, shoulders slumping. "I'm so scared," he confessed.

"I know you are." I gestured him forward.

He took one step and then another. His eyes looked up into mine, the fire gone from them. "You understand, don't you? I couldn't let her go."

I wrapped my arms around him. "I understand," I said.

Reality crashed back into existence around me. I reached out for the wood of the door frame, trying to reassure myself that it was real and not just a product of my imagination. My other hand went to the pendant around my neck.

The metal warmed my fingers. *Richard?* I asked.

Before he answered, a hand—a paw—fell on my shoulder. "Jae?"

I turned to Czoltan. Emotion overwhelmed me and I grabbed him in as tight an embrace as I could manage.

What...what did I do? Richard's voice fluttered through my consciousness.

I didn't answer him right away because Czoltan made a noise as I squeezed the air from his lungs and then hugged me right back, pressing the side of his muzzle to my face. His whiskers tickled me and I loved it.

You let your emotions overwhelm you. Like a ghost, I told Richard, holding tight to Czoltan. *I'm sorry.*

"Jae—it is you, right?" Czoltan asked.

"It's me."

He growled against me. "Tell me something only you would know."

So I told him exactly what we did in the supply tent and how many times we did it. He huffed in surprise and then the movement of his hips told me that his tail was wagging.

"You did it," he said. "You bound him."

I held up the pendant. "He's here. I'm talking to him now."

Richard sounded more like the captain I remembered now that he'd accepted the steadying of my mind. *You're going to take me to the police now.*

Yes.

"How is he?" Czoltan asked.

Can I see Desiree first? One last time?

"He wants to see Desiree again."

"Oof. Is that a good idea?"

I wondered that too. "I don't think he can hurt her."

"You don't think..."

I won't, Richard said. *I promise.*

"Let's think about it," I said, and took a step down the hall. My legs gave out and I had to cling to Czoltan. "But first maybe I need a drink."

"Water? Or..."

There's scotch in the cabinet, Richard told me.

"Water."

So we went to the kitchen and I got a glass of water, which I drank with shaking hands while sitting at their kitchen table. Czoltan sat with me, keeping quiet, but I knew he wanted to ask me about the binding.

When he spoke, though, it wasn't about that. "Sergei guessed you were going to use the story of our breakup," he said without looking at me.

"Of course he did." I focused on the cool water and eradicating the dryness from my mouth.

"Was that the story you bound him with?"

"No."

He waited for me to elaborate, and when I didn't, he said, "I guess what I don't understand..." He laced his fingers together and stared down at them. "If you felt like losing me was so painful—painful enough that you could relate to a ghost who'd been separated from his wife by being killed—why didn't you just come back?"

"It sounds so easy when you just say it." I finished the glass and got up to refill it, pleased that my legs worked. "But if it were that easy, I wouldn't have given you up in the first place."

"So why did you? And don't say your family. Sergei told me—"

"I know." I paced back and forth with my glass. "Fear. I probably should've pushed harder to get an appointment with one of those VA therapists."

You'd still be waiting, Richard chimed in dryly.

I ignored him, took a breath, and tried to organize my thoughts. "I saw love and life ending in the worst way I can imagine. There was nowhere to run away from it, trapped on that bus. It stays with you. Everything in your life has that shadow at the back of it. I know you're not going to end up dying of K-118 on a bus in Kosovo. But odds are one of us dies before the other."

"Sure. But until then, we'd still have that time."

"I know." I sat back down and put my hand over his paw. "In the dream-story, you died. And I felt crushed that we'd missed that time. That's what I didn't see on the bus, all the life those people had before the end. That matters too."

He turned his paw to clasp my hand. "I guess the story worked."

"Sort of. I mean, it got a little...twisted around. He made me see things a little differently than I had been."

More truthfully, Richard corrected.

Sure.

Tell him, he ordered.

Czoltan asked, "Differently good or bad?"

"More truthfully," I said. "I don't think I realized how afraid I was of...something terrible happening. How afraid Richard was of being alone, of going into death without Desiree."

Czoltan scratched the base of an ear. "That sounds tough."

"It helps to know what to call it." I finished the water. "We can keep talking about this on the way to the hospital."

CHAPTER 10
THE NEXT JOB

C zoltan asked me more about the binding on the way to the hospital. I answered as best I could, but I know it got confusing when I couldn't tell him which parts had been invented by me and which by Richard. Richard probably didn't know any more than I did; he stayed silent and I didn't push him.

Even though I enjoyed talking to Czoltan, I missed Sergei. At this point it probably wouldn't have hurt for me to swap Richard's pendant for Sergei's ring, but with Richard being newly dead and even more newly bound, I wanted him to have someone familiar to talk to in case he started to freak out.

He didn't, at least not out loud, not even when I called the police to have someone meet us at the hospital to take custody of him. There were a lot of questions, including the standard "Do you know" set: "Do you know how much trouble you could be in, do you know the penalty for interfering in police business, do you know how dangerous ghosts are," and so on. I answered "yes" to all of them.

When I hung up the phone, Czoltan turned to me. "Are you going to be arrested again?"

"Hope not." I tapped the pendant. "Once we transfer the binding over, they'll be able to get a confession to go along with my video evidence, which frankly might be a little shaky. I'm not sure whether Michigan is a two-party recording state."

"What?"

"Illinois requires consent of all the parties on a recording for it to be legal. California does too, and there are a bunch of others, but I haven't memorized which is which because I operate out of Illinois so I always have to get everyone's consent. I didn't get Richard's before I recorded him, but if Michigan only requires that one person know about the recording, it might be okay."

"Oh. If he's bound, he has to tell the truth, right?" He paused. "Sergei says he must tell the truth when you compel him to, but that he can bend it if you're not specifically ordering him to be truthful, and also that he can lie to me even if I tell him not to." His ears flicked.

"Sergei, tell the truth," I ordered.

Czoltan smiled and leaned back in the car seat. "He sounds very mournful right now."

"He would, the old bear. Ask him why he doesn't appear here in the car."

"He says it's very small and there would be no room."

"For his insubstantial form."

"That's right. He says, 'you would not want my head to stick up above roof.'"

"Actually," I said, turning into a parking garage near the hospital, "that sounds pretty entertaining."

Captain Waters, the Detroit PD's ghost specialist, met us in the hospital lobby along with Sergeant Jefferson, whom I'd talked to at the precinct where I'd been arrested. Waters shook my hand when I introduced myself. "Tackling a renegade ghost by yourself takes some chops."

Jefferson, taller than her companion, kept her arms folded and shook her head. "Takes a damn idiot is what it takes," she said. "I could arrest you on half a dozen charges."

"Yeah, but they probably wouldn't stick," I said. "At worst, you could fine me for not checking in with the police before working a case, which would be fair, but I could argue that because the case technically began when Richard hired me to come out here, the case started in Illinois and my Illinois license permits me to follow it across state lines if need be. I don't plan to take up residency here and I caught you an attempted murderer."

"I'm process-focused, not results-focused," she said. "Lucky for you our chief is results-focused. All right, he wants to see his wife one more time before we take him in, right? You think there's any danger in that?" I shook my head. "Let's go then."

Czoltan looked at the doorway we'd come in through. "Aren't hospitals ghost-proofed?"

Jefferson had already started walking to the elevator. Over her shoulder, she said, "They can turn off the protection in certain rooms."

We rode up to the fourth floor and signed in amid the smell of antiseptic and disinfectant. Desiree was only allowed two visitors at a time, so Czoltan stayed outside with Sergeant Jefferson while Captain Waters and I walked in.

Desiree lay on the bed with an IV in one arm and a heart monitor hooked up to her. She looked fully human, just as she had the last time I'd seen her; even though she'd been turned, she wouldn't transform while unconscious.

Richard manifested next to the bed, standing and looking down at his widow. "She looks peaceful," he said.

"They'll be keeping her sedated for a little while. The change is stressful on the body and it's best if you can sleep it off."

"I wish I could talk to her. Tell her I'm sorry." His voice remained rough and low.

"I'll explain to her. And maybe Captain Waters will let you make a recorded message for her."

"We can work that out," Waters said.

Richard turned to us and nodded. "Thank you," he said. "I'd like to stay for a moment longer, if that's all right."

Waters nodded. "As long as you need."

When he was ready, he dematerialized and we left the room, walking out into the brightly-lit hospital hallway.

To my surprise, next to Jefferson and Czoltan in the hospital waiting area sat a brawny man, bald, leaning forward with his hands around his head while Czoltan patted his shoulder and said something to him. Whatever it was, it helped, because the man sat up and exhaled, and then saw me.

He sprang to his feet and came toward me so quickly that my defense mechanisms tensed me, pushing me a step back before I recognized that he wasn't coming at me aggressively. He spread his arms and wrapped them around me. "Thank you," he said. "I'm so, so sorry."

Lupine smell tickled my nose. "Galen?" I guessed.

He stepped back and nodded. "Yeah. I went human to come to the hospital. Figured it'd be easier on them." Czoltan snorted, his wolf's muzzle smiling at me over Galen's shoulder. "Anyway, dude, I am so sorry about trying to, uh, arrest you."

"Arrest" clearly wasn't the word he would've used if Captain Waters wasn't standing beside me. "It's fine," I said. "There was a warrant."

"I should've checked." He ducked his head as we walked back to join the others. "And you saved her life."

"Well, technically you did," I reminded him. "I just told you how."

He laughed, a little too loudly. The nurse at the desk looked up, then went back to her computer. "Yeah, I did. They said she's gonna be fine, and she'll be a werewolf, of course, but her body's doing okay. Uh, when she wakes up, I'm gonna—I'm gonna ask her to move in."

I touched Richard's pendant. "I've got her husband's ghost here, so—"

"Oh shit!" His eyes widened and he backed away. "I'm just —I'm gonna go sit with her. They said I could when you came out. Sorry. Again." And with that, he hurried down the corridor and disappeared into Desiree's room.

Captain Waters cleared her throat at that point. "Maybe this would be a good time for me to take possession of the ghost?"

You okay? I asked Richard.

He didn't reply for a few seconds and then said, *I think I will be. It's...good to see someone caring for her. I can't anymore.*

All right. I'm going to give you to this nice woman here, okay?

Sergeant, I know what's happening. I'm not a child just because I'm dead.

I know, sir, I said. *I'm really sorry about what happened. It's been my privilege to serve under you and a great pleasure to know you as a friend.*

Leaving out the part where I tried to have you killed, he said.

At least you failed.

True, he said. *You're better than I gave you credit for. Remember that, will you?*

I'll try.

I pulled the pendant off my neck and gave it to Captain Waters. "Should we do the transfer here? I've never done one before."

She looked around the waiting area. "Let's see if they have an empty room we can use for five minutes."

I'm pretty sure that if I'd asked, the answer would have been no, but a police badge works wonders in a hospital. Some hospitals. A nurse brought the two of us to an empty room, where Captain Waters assured him (and Jefferson and Czoltan) we'd be out in ten minutes.

The spell was a simple one as best I could tell, and Waters knew it without referring to a book or phone, which made me feel a little inadequate until I remembered that that wasn't actually my job. I didn't feel anything as the binding was transferred, but when it was done, Captain Waters said, "Hello, Richard." She stared into space for a moment and then asked me, "What did you use to bind him?"

So I told her in brief the story of fear and loss, which was easier without Czoltan in the room. She nodded and looked over my shoulder into space for a moment. "I can keep that connection," she said. "We'll conduct a couple interviews and then we'll try to find a resolution for him."

"Meaning," I said, "you'll find him someone else to bind to?"

She didn't meet my eyes. "If possible."

I took Sergei back in the lobby of the hospital on our way out. *Hello, old bear.*

Show me the binding, he asked, so I went through my memories of it as the rest of the conversation went on.

"Do you think Richard will be all right?" Czoltan asked.

"Honestly? I think they'll banish him. A ghost who nearly killed someone, who used bioweapons? He's too dangerous to keep around."

Sergei and Czoltan both took a moment to process that. Czoltan spoke first. "Banishing—so that's like killing him. Wouldn't they have to have a trial?"

"Ghosts have no rights," I said at the same time as Sergei said it in my mind. "He's not considered a person, so it's more like—putting down an animal who attacked a person."

"But if he's bound, he's stable, so he's not a threat anymore," Czoltan protested.

"They might not banish him," I said to both him and Sergei. "Ghosts are useful."

I finished reviewing the binding in my mind. *You did well,* the bear said.

"Sergei sounded like a real person when I was talking to him," the wolf said. We walked across the parking lot to the car under gathering clouds as I tried not to think about having said good-bye to Richard.

"You should know how hard it is for extras to have rights."

"Sure, but..." He spread his paws. "Ghosts don't get included in that. They were human."

"So 'were' you. The method of transformation is just different." This line of discussion made me a little uncomfortable with Sergei listening. "Look, I agree with you, for what it's worth. I think ghosts should be treated as children rather than animals. They need a guardian, but with that guardian they should have certain rights. But they don't have anyone agitating for their rights at the moment. If there are bad guardians, you don't hear about them."

I have a list of complaints.

I do too, come to that, I replied.

Czoltan looked back up at the hospital. "It's just hard to think of Captain Collison like...like that."

"I know. He was my friend. And he died."

We got to the car, Czoltan still chewing on that. "I know

it's weird," I continued. "Sergei died a hundred years ago. We have this fixed idea that death is the end, and we shouldn't expect anything to go on after that. And yet, for the last couple hundred years, we've been learning more and more about ghosts. It just hasn't caught up to the way we think in a lot of places yet. Ghosts feel like artifacts, like not the real thing, when in fact—I mean, Sergei's lived longer as a ghost than he did as a werebear."

Perhaps not if you count time captive but not bound to person.

As we pulled out of the parking lot, Czoltan said, "I never thought about it that way. I mean, my family's—you know. Why didn't they stick around? Didn't they have something to keep them to the world?"

"Maybe they did. There's theories that there are a lot more ghosts than we know, that many of them are out there for a while but then either resolve their business or come to some sort of peace on their own before the living world notices them."

The wolf turned his muzzle to the car window, staring at the buildings, and I'm pretty sure I was thinking the same thing he was: what if those old windows were hiding a bunch of ghosts? "That's sad," he said. "I hope my family are at peace now."

"I'm sure they are."

I have not noticed very many other ghosts, Sergei said.

Would you notice them?

If I were looking.

Can you hide from other ghosts?

He didn't answer. I pulled onto the highway and Czoltan's attention came back to me. "What are you going to do now?"

I'd been wondering the same thing, specifically about him. Now that we'd reconnected, it didn't feel possible to go back to the way things had been (not talking at all). But he didn't want

203

to be long-distance friends and neither of us wanted to commit to anything more yet, so moving cities would be moving way too fast (right?). So where did that leave us?

"I'm going to take you home," I said.

"I meant—"

"I know what you meant. That's as far ahead as I want to plan right at the moment."

He gave an amused huff. "All right."

So we drove to Wolftown in silence—external, at least.

So you got very chummy with him, I said to Sergei.

He wanted to talk.

You're not compelled to.

I wanted to. He was so polite.

You're interfering again.

Perhaps next time you will not leave me out of dangerous situation. I could have helped you.

Or you could have messed up the binding spell. I don't know how those things work. Maybe Richard could have taken over your spirit, or something. I didn't want to risk it.

Pah, risk. You lose ghost, you get new one.

Have you not been listening to this conversation?

Yes, I listen. You have nice sentiment but is not reality, da?

What should I do about Czoltan? I asked, to change the subject.

You know answer to this.

Pretend I don't.

You take him home. Ask him to go upstairs. Then fuck him. Is simple.

You would think after four years you would know that sex isn't as simple as it was when you were alive. If we have sex then that implies that we're going to stay close.

He gave the ghost equivalent of a sigh. *Jae, listen to me. I tell you very important truth.*

This should be good. *Go ahead.*

Four years I have watched you date. You date werewolves even though you know there is no future, because if there was future it would be with this one. You date humans and you are disappointed because they are not werewolves.

That's not true. I could date a human.

You are disappointed because they are not this werewolf. You are in love with him. And he is in love with you. Look at what he goes through today to help you, to stay by your side. Risks his life.

He's a good guy, and I was in trouble and needed him.

And he is in love with you.

I took the exit for Wolftown. *Even assuming you're right, what can we do about it? Nothing's changed.*

Everything has changed.

What?

You have not thought about the binding you told with Richard?

I mean...I've thought about how close I came to losing it.

You did not end your relationship with Czoltan because you were afraid of your family rejecting him.

Well, you weren't there, so—

You ended it because you were afraid of losing him. Or, perhaps, you were afraid of leaving him alone.

Was it that simple? The memories of Breg-lumi had shaken me for sure, especially presented as realistically as Richard had made them. The prospect of going upstairs with Czoltan held a lot of appeal, especially as the adrenaline of following this case wore off, if only just to have his arms around me.

Arms, or whatever, Sergei said.

I snorted. Czoltan looked over at me and his ears flicked. "Sergei?"

"Yeah."

"What's he—you know, it's none of my business."

I pulled into the Wolftown parking lot and opened my door. "Just catching up," I said.

"You're coming in?" Czoltan got out the other side and eyed me.

"I thought I'd walk you back to your house. You went out of your way for me. It's the least I can do."

"Jae."

"Maybe we could grab dinner? I need to stick around for a couple more days for the police."

He gathered in a breath that felt like it was going to be a rejection. Then his ears came up and he smiled and said, "Sure. Dinner sounds fine."

So we walked together through Wolftown security, where I was pulled aside for a ghost check again and Sergei grumbled about it again. Czoltan watched with a little amusement and rejoined me when I got through.

"Does that happen every time?"

"Every single time. But it's worth it."

Thank you, Sergei said with a little sarcasm.

It was interesting coming back to the plaza in Wolftown Detroit without having to worry about warrant officers hunting me. I appreciated the freedom, and when I found the building I'd jumped off of, my hand went down to my leg and the injury I'd suffered and I thanked God that my only souvenir of that jump was a limp.

Czoltan strolled down one of the main boulevards, in no particular hurry, and I followed at his side. In the hospital, Czoltan had gotten stares; now I was back to being the one stared at. But I didn't care. I worked through the situation in my head and factored in how nice it felt to be strolling through Wolftown with Czoltan at my side.

When I thought about a more permanent arrangement with him, anxiety spiked in me, but now I recognized what it was. It grasped for rationale and found family, but heck, my mother didn't want to hear about my work in Wolftown and I already edited my life for her benefit. There would come a time when there'd have to be a reckoning, but I could push that down the road. If Sergei was right and fear was what was keeping me from this, then maybe all I had to do was take a deep breath and a step forward.

We turned down a side street and I recognized his neighborhood. Another street and there was his townhouse, lined up amid all the others but looking very distinct to me. We walked up to the front door and he said, "Well, I'm home."

I took his paw. "You are." He kept looking into my face, and I looked back at his, and I said, "Do you mind if I come in?"

He raised an eyebrow. "I thought we were going to get dinner."

"It's six-thirty." Somehow it was only six-thirty. It felt like I'd lived three days since I'd returned to Wolftown Detroit.

"Closer to seven. When do you eat dinner?"

"Anytime between seven-thirty and eleven, depending on how much work I have."

He snorted. "We usually eat around seven."

"All right, so...mind if I come in for half an hour? Is your roommate home?"

"Probably." Czoltan exhaled. "Fine, okay."

I took a step back. "If you don't want me to come in, that's fine. We can say good-bye here on the front porch. But I want to talk a bit, and I'd rather do that inside."

He shook his head and gave me a little smile. "All right. Come on in."

Smooth, Sergei said as I followed Czoltan in through the front door, closing it behind me.

The roommate, Tari, a sturdier, shorter, and darker wolf than Czoltan, was sprawled on the couch in the living room lazily playing some first-person shooter game. "Hey, Zo," he said as we walked in, and then his ears perked up and he whipped his head around to stare at me. "Hey, I remember you," he said. "You were here this morning."

"Someone's shooting at you," I said, nodding at the screen.

"Fuck!" He paused the game and set the controller down. "Sorry."

"I'm Jae," I said.

"Jae's had a day," Czoltan said. "We're gonna chill a bit and then go to dinner."

"Oh, cool. Hey, do you want to grab tacos? I could go for some tacos."

Czoltan met my eyes, and after a moment said, "I could grab you some on the way back, sure."

"No, I mean—" Tari's ears flicked as his eyes went from Czoltan to me. "Ohhh. Gotcha. Yeah, if you could, that'd be great, thanks. I'd come with, but," he gestured at the screen, "I've been trying to take this base for a week and I'm so close now."

"No problem," Czoltan said, and then took a step toward the staircase. "You want to come upstairs?"

This was to me, of course, and even as Sergei barked approval into my mind I said, "Sure," and we padded up to his bedroom.

He left the door open, which Sergei commented on, but he did invite me to sit down on the bed with him. So I sat close, and it was nice just sitting there with him, even if I didn't quite dare lean against him the way I'd used to.

I didn't want to say anything at first, just enjoying the stillness of the room (with the muted sounds of shooting from downstairs). But then Czoltan said, "What did you want to talk about?" so I put together thoughts in my head.

Tell him you want to get back together, Sergei supplied.

I'm getting there, I said.

"First of all...I really wanted to thank you for everything you did today. God knows you have plenty of reasons to tell me to go to hell, and you didn't. I'd probably be dead today without you. Desiree for sure would be. So...thank you."

"You're welcome." His tail gave one thwap on the bed. "I mean, anyone would've helped you in that situation. I don't think I did anything—"

"You did." I put a hand on his paw and rubbed there gently.

He looked down but didn't move his paw away. "What's second?"

"Second is that I missed you. I miss you, I mean. It's been a long time but I hope that today showed you that I haven't stopped thinking about you. Even when I didn't know I was thinking about you."

Czoltan nodded slowly, guardedly. "Forgive me, but missing me doesn't do me any good."

"No, I know. That's the other thing. I think—"

'We should get naked right now.' Say it.

Hush.

In my day we did not need all this preamble. When I met my wife I said 'I would like to bed you' and she said 'I would also like that,' and so we did.

"I think I need to go back to therapy for a bit. There's a lot I haven't worked out around relationships and stuff. I don't think I was..." I stopped myself. "I wasn't entirely honest with you about why we broke up. But if it helps, I wasn't entirely honest with myself either."

He didn't say anything, but his ears perked a little more toward me. I looked down at my hand on his paw, skin atop fur. My heart sped up. Excitement, maybe? Panic, maybe? I forced the words out. "This is part of what I have to figure out,

209

but I think it was just fear, a kind of PTSD where I'm afraid to get close to anyone."

Ahem.

"Except Sergei, but that's because I control that relationship. And I know if something happened to me, someone else would claim him. He wouldn't really miss me."

That is not true, and besides I was saying that you take credit for my idea.

"Sergei came up with that idea, actually," I amended. "The binding story—what Richard and I went through, it was hard for us both. And I don't want to end up like Richard, so afraid of death that I become a ghost."

"I don't want that either," Czoltan said. "Who would?"

"But I think...I know...I want you to be part of my life."

He was quiet, and then he shifted his paw to interlace his fingers with mine. "So how is that going to work? Neither of us can pull up and move."

"Is that a 'yes'?" My heart sped up.

The smile grew more pronounced on his muzzle. "I've missed you too. And if we're approaching this knowing what the mistakes were last time and with a plan to make them better this time, then yes."

I leaned over and gave him a quick kiss on the side of the muzzle. "It's very sweet for you to say 'we,' but it was mostly my fault—"

He grabbed my chin and kissed me full on the lips, the way we used to kiss, warm with a little bit of bumping of teeth as his big canines got in the way. His breath was a little sour from not having eaten or drunk anything in a while, but I didn't care at all.

"Mmm," I said when we parted, my eyes on his. "That was nice."

"I made mistakes too," Czoltan said. "I was younger. I

expected you to be this perfect boyfriend, and when you weren't I got angry at you and gave up."

"I wanted to be perfect."

"Yeah, but you can't be. Hey, I went through a lot because of the war, too. I'm seeing a counselor still. Losing my family was hard."

"I know." I pushed away thoughts of my own family.

"The point is." He nuzzled my face, and that was warmer and more intimate than the kiss somehow. "I know about doing the work and I'll support you. But you still haven't answered my question. Do you move? Do I move?"

I shook my head. "If we want to be with each other...it's been a long day. I don't want to think about the details right now. I just want to be with you."

"I guess that sounds okay." He smiled, and his tail thumped against the bed several more times.

The wagging made me smile, so I leaned up and kissed him again, and this time we held it longer, his paw reaching around my back to hold me. I leaned into his body, breathing the scent of his fur fully and letting myself fall back to happier times. Those times could come again.

Jae. I must speak with you.

I sighed. *Right now?*

Right now.

He became visible before I gave permission, standing in front of the bedroom door so that he nearly filled the room.

Czoltan leaned away from me slightly. "We weren't going to do anything," he said a little too quickly. "If you're planning on watching."

"This is not to watch," Sergei said before I could add my own objection. "This is to speak to both of you at once."

"All right," I said. "What's so important?"

Sergei hadn't become quite all the way visible, I noticed; I could see the glint of the doorknob through his bare brown-furred stomach. He looked steadily at me. "I am moving on," he said. "My connection to this world is fading."

"What?" I sat up straight, and Czoltan's arm fell away from me.

"It is true." The bear shook his head mournfully. "I believe it was what you said about viewing death through the lens of the life that preceded it." He held his ghostly paws out, their outlines fading still more. "I think of my wife now with joy for the life we had, not with sadness for the last moments we missed. I did not know that would release me, and I want to thank you for it."

"Oh my God." Czoltan rested a paw on my shoulder.

I swallowed, not sure how to respond to this. I was happy for Sergei, but... "I'm going to miss you, old bear," I said. "I don't know how I'll get along without you."

"You will find another ghost," he said. "We are easily replaceable."

I had to swallow again, and even when I did my voice was husky. "Not so easily," I said. "Not after four years. I'm gonna have to teach someone the job all over again?"

"You taught an old bear," he said with kindness. "This time, look for a ghost born less than a century ago?"

"Good advice." I leaned against Czoltan.

"Thank you," the wolf said to Sergei. "I mean, you saved his life a bunch and you brought us back together."

The bear's outlines had definitely faded everywhere except around his head. "I should thank you for welcoming Jae back to your life," he said. "He has also been special to me, but now I know I do not leave him alone." He spread faint paws. "Four years it took me to bring him back to you."

"Jesus, Sergei." I wanted to stand up and hug him, but

there was precious little left to hug, and what there was wasn't even substantial.

"It could be." He smiled at me. "I will know soon enough, *da*?"

"Good-bye," I said as his head faded away.

Even when he was gone, his voice echoed in my head one last time. *Remember what you discovered inside yourself,* he said. *Do not let fear keep you from it.*

I won't, I said back, but he didn't reply. *Sergei?*

Still nothing. I called his name a few more times, trying to convince myself that he was playing a joke, that he'd be back with a hearty laugh and a "ha ha, you cannot get rid of a Russian this easily." But there was nothing but my own thoughts in my head, and it took only a few seconds for me to realize what a lonely place that was.

And then the paw on my shoulder squeezed gently. "Is he gone?" Czoltan asked.

"I...I think so. I can't hear him anymore."

The paw slid across my back to hug me. "I'm sorry."

I rested my head against his shoulder. "It's—I don't know how to deal with it right now."

Czoltan nodded. For a short time we just sat there together. Then he said, "Weird day, huh?"

For whatever reason, that set me off. It started as a small giggle in my stomach, and I said, "The weirdest," and then I couldn't stop laughing.

Czoltan giggled with me, and then as my laughter didn't stop, he held me tighter and asked, "Are you all right?"

"Yeah." I wiped my eyes. "I don't know. It's all a bit much. I came here today to look after an old friend's wife, and I ended up almost dying, fighting with my ex, saving someone's life, binding a ghost, and getting back together with the person I never stopped caring about, and now I've lost the closest friend I had for the last four years with like a minute's warning. Everything's turned on its head, you know?"

"I know." He nuzzled me. "I wouldn't have thought when I got up this morning that I'd see you again, much less witness a transformation and a ghost binding before ending up back here in my bedroom with you."

"I don't mind where it ended up, except for it's weird without Sergei. And it's going to be weird for a while, I think."

"I can imagine. Or—" He shook his head. "Maybe I can't. It's like losing a twin brother, maybe?"

"Maybe something like that." I rested my paw on his thigh again. "But he's leaving me in good hands. Good paws."

"Yeah." Czoltan squeezed me again.

After another moment, he said, "Why don't we go get something to eat? Then maybe later, if you feel like it, you could come back and..." He cleared his throat. "I'd like it if you stayed here tonight."

"Yeah." I didn't have to think about it. "I'd like that too."

———————

We went out to a Korean barbecue place near his house. It wasn't the place we'd gone years ago, but that place was gone, and anyway, we both thought it was about time we started some new memories. The kimchi was good, the beef a little tough, but it was the best meal I'd had in a while.

"I'll check in at the police station tomorrow and see if they need me to testify," I said as we waited for the check to arrive. "Might end up coming back here a fair amount, depending on how the case goes. Though I don't imagine Desiree will want to press charges."

"You don't need an excuse to come back now," Czoltan reminded me.

"I know. But..."

"Jae. I want to come to Chicago, too. And in a few months we'll see how things are going. I'm sure we'll have a feeling about where we want to go, if we want to take another step."

"If? There's no 'if.' Sergei moved on because he believed we were set up for good."

"Uh huh." The wolf nodded. "And he's gone now. What matters isn't that we stay together forever, but that whatever we do, we do for the right reasons. Maybe we'll find we've grown to be different people in four years. If that happens, we'll both know it, and we can at least stay friends."

I licked the spicy taste of gochujang off my lips. "I hope it doesn't come to that."

"Me too. But I don't want to invest all of who I am into this relationship working out. That's how you end up a ghost."

"Mmm."

"Plus," he said with a grin, "it'll give you a lot of time to figure out how to tell your mother."

"Right," I sighed. "I guess I'll have to figure that one out, too." I took the check as the waiter approached. Czoltan reached for his wallet, but I waved him off. "No, no. I can still expense this."

"To whom?"

I gave my credit card to the waiter. When he'd gone, I said. "Richard's estate? I don't know. I can write it off my taxes, and besides, you went over and above the call of duty today. This is just the beginning of me paying you back."

"All right," he said, "but I don't want you to feel you have to keep paying me back for months."

"Oh, I know. I—"

"But the rest of tonight is fine."

I smiled and stood, and he stood with me. "You got it," I said, and together we left the restaurant to walk home.

EPILOGUE

I t turned out to be two days before the hospital let me in to see Desiree. I wasn't immediate family, so she had to be conscious enough to agree to a visit. I did send her an email explaining the false warrant and including a couple statements from the police, and she replied that she was terribly sorry for having thought about shooting me.

I didn't mind staying the extra day or two, for obvious reasons. The Detroit police didn't mind either, and they took advantage of my presence to get a more detailed statement. I put in almost a full work day with Officer Pulaski, including a two-hour session with the Department of Extranormal Relations, where I had to affirm to a very stern gentleman no fewer than five times that yes, I did understand the laws surrounding transformations, and that just because in this one case I'd managed to narrowly stay within the law (his words), I shouldn't go imagining that I could oversee any other transformations.

When he'd gone, Officer Pulaski shifted to wolf and growled. "What a dick."

"He's just doing his job." I was glad that she felt comfortable enough to be in wolf form around me.

"He's enjoying his job a little too much." She set her ears back.

"Really? Didn't look like he was enjoying any part of this."

"This whole stigma around transformation, all the laws around it. There's still prejudice, y'know? They say everything's fine, we're all equal, but ninety percent of us live inside walled cities—"

"I heard seventy-five."

"And these DER idiots have their noses up the ass of any transformation unless you file their paperwork in triplicate with a video testimony from the extra swearing that they're not drunk or high and they really want to become a werewolf. Or a kumiho or a kishi or an encantado. Like they can't fathom why anyone would do this of their own volition."

I struggled to find a reasonable line without contradicting her passion. "Sure, there's still fear, but it is an irreversible decision, so doesn't it make sense to double-check so you don't, you know, drunk transform or something?"

She pointed at me. "That right there, that 'irreversible' bullshit. That's part of it."

I blinked. "Is it not irreversible? I thought I was pretty up on the news."

"It is, but the way people say 'irreversible' makes it sound like a spinal cord injury. Sure, once you're a werewolf you can't be human again, but it's not like your life is over, is it? You can still work, you can still get married. You've got a place to live."

"I guess so. But I mean, don't you think that the Wolftowns are a good compromise? Extras get to define their own society in safety?"

"Don't get me started." She waved a thick paw. "No, they're not a good compromise. The way to break down preju-

TIM SUSMAN

dice is to expose people to each other. Wolftown lets humans forget about extras, compartmentalize them into 'those' people who live in 'those' places. We need to be out among them."

"We tried that."

"Back in the forties and fifties. We tried a lot of things that didn't work back then. Did we abandon them forever?" She stopped and gave a short laugh. "Sorry. Didn't mean to bore you with my activism."

"It's fine," I said. "I'm—I'm dating a werewolf, so I want to know about this. What the current thinking is, all that."

She gave me a splayed-ear raised eyebrow. "Not the woman in the hospital?"

"No, the other werewolf who was with us. Not the one who bit her, the other one."

"Oh." Her ears came back upright. "Good for you. Good for you both."

"I sure hope so."

When I did finally get to visit Desiree, she was seeing a Transition Specialist and had shifted to half-wolf. Her brown fur and black-tipped ears looked nothing like the human she'd been, but when she turned my way, there was something familiar in her brown eyes. "Hi, Jae," she said. "Marco and I are about done."

Marco nodded and stood. "You're doing very well." He gave me an appraising look as he walked toward the door. "I'll see you tomorrow."

When we were alone, Desiree said, "Should I change back to human?"

I glanced at her bare white chest ruff. "Er, no, that's fine."

She smiled. "Good. I want to stay in this form as much as I can. It takes a little getting used to. I itch all over, kind of."

"I remember some of the Kosovans who'd been changed saying that." I pulled up a chair to sit beside the bed.

"But I don't suppose you're here to talk about the transformation."

"No." I took out my phone. "Do you mind if I record this?"

She shook her head. "But I want to say, before you start—thank you for saving my life."

"Oh. You're welcome." It felt awkward, because what else was I supposed to do? But at the same time, I guess I did risk a lot to save her. So did Galen, though, and Czoltan. "It was a team effort."

"I owe you."

"Don't worry about it." I could see she wanted to worry about it, so I started the recording. "Jae Kim in Detroit General Hospital with Desiree Collison, following up on Richard Collison's case." I gave the date and time and then said, "Desiree, you're okay with this conversation being recorded?"

"Yes, I am."

"Okay. Sorry, Promise we won't stay that formal. I just need to do it for the tape."

"It's fine."

"So." I took a breath. "Can you tell me when Richard died?"

"It was January fourteenth of this year."

"And how did it happen?"

"He had a heart attack shoveling snow."

"Did you find him?"

She laughed, a little shaky. "He found me. I was playing a video game and he walked into the room. I said, 'I thought you were outside,' and he said, 'I am.'"

"It must have been difficult."

"Not terribly. I mean, storing his body was hard because I

219

had to do it by myself." She caught my look. "It's in the cellar, wrapped in cloth. I tried to preserve it as best I could."

"He wanted that?"

"He insisted. I wanted to report his death, but he said it would make things difficult. He wanted to wrap up some loose ends before he moved on. I didn't know as much about ghosts then. I thought he could do that."

"And when did your relationship with Galen start?"

She looked away from me, out the window. "A couple years ago."

"Oh."

"Yeah." She turned back with a small smile on her muzzle. "Not quite the perfect wife, huh? But it wasn't anything serious, not at the time. Richard was—well, let's be honest, he didn't want to have sex as often as I did. For a month, you can stand it, but after a year, after two..." She teased claws through the fur of her stomach. "I met Galen through a Spouses of Veterans group. His wife served in Afghanistan and she...she took her own life. He wanted an idea of what she'd been going through."

"Ah, shit. I'm sorry."

"Yeah. You can see where we might have a lot to talk about. And—well, you've seen him."

"Mostly when I saw him he was shooting at me, but—yeah."

"I didn't tell Richard. I guess he suspected, though. That's why you're here?"

I nodded. "He hired me to follow you."

"And then he put out a fake warrant on you? He was trying to kill you?"

"Yes." I looked down.

"Ghosts get lost," she said. "I know that. I thought I was keeping him grounded. I'm sorry I didn't manage it better."

"It's not your fault," I said. "It takes training and magic. But..." I took a breath. "There was more to it."

I'd pushed myself off the edge so now I'd have to tell her, but it still took me long enough to get the nerve up that she had to prod me. "Jae?"

I looked her in the eye. "Richard maybe wanted to kill me, but he definitely tried to kill you. They—they found K-118 in your bloodstream."

She frowned slightly but didn't say anything. I went on. "K-118 is a bioweapon from the war that gooses your metabolism and puts it into a vicious spiral until your heart gives out. Problem is, it needs a jump start. Stress of war is a good one, running for your life is another."

Now her brow cleared. "Or chasing a suspected serial killer."

"It almost worked. Thank you for not shooting me."

"Thank you for saving my life. How did you know about the bioweapon?"

So I turned off the recorder and told her about Kosovo, though not about Breg-lumi; nobody should have that in their memory if they don't need it there. "I was reminded of it while talking to Czoltan and then I remembered that you'd been sweating an awful lot, and there was a point where I knew Richard had access to it."

"You put all that together while you were being hunted for being a serial killer?"

I gave her a crooked smile. "I'd found a place to hide and rest. I was doing all I could to get rid of the warrant, so of course I started wondering how it had happened. There weren't many people who knew I was going to be in Detroit that day, so once I was sure it was Richard, the rest fell into place."

"Your place to hide was with...what's his name, Czoltan? Your ex?"

"Yeah. Actually, Czoltan and I are...we're back together again. Trying, anyway."

Her ears came all the way up. "Good luck."

"It's funny." I clasped my hands together. "I had a ghost, Sergei. He was my best friend for four years, and somehow, me getting back together with Czoltan helped him resolve his ghostly issues. He moved on. For real."

"That's good," Desiree said. "I'm glad even a little good came out of this." Her ears flicked. "I think Galen's going to stick around too."

"Glad to hear it." It wasn't my place to tell her what he'd told me in confidence. I stood. "Hey, let's keep in touch, okay? You're going through a transition and if you need a friend to talk to...y'know, just call. I know we didn't talk much back in the day, but we've been through a pretty rough time together."

"No friends like army friends," Desiree said with a smile. "Sure thing. I've got your number."

I held up a hand and headed for the door. I hadn't quite gotten there when Desiree said, "Jae?"

"Yeah?" I turned.

"What's going to happen to Richard?"

"Oh." I leaned back against the door. "The police have him. I guess he'll go to someone who needs a ghost if they decide not to banish him."

Those eyes again, staring at me. "You need a ghost."

"Oh, no," I said. "No, I—"

"You caught him."

I gave a nervous laugh. "Who told you?"

"The lawyers. Well, just one, but there are two working on it—anyway, now that Richard's dead there's an estate to worry about and the police notified his executor and she called me and gave me a few details along the way. In the case where someone's a ghost, technically I would have a say in where they go as the next of kin, but because Richard is charged in a criminal case the police get to decide."

"Right."

"And if they banish him, is that the same as moving on?"

"Nobody knows." I sighed. "Some ghosts choose it because there isn't a better option. Some are terrified of it."

"What do you think?"

I shook my head. "I don't know."

"But what do you *think*?"

I didn't want to have this conversation, but I couldn't lie to her. "I think...I think it's not the same. I think it just...erases them."

She nodded and turned her eyes forward, staring at the wall. "I know I owe you so much, but I want to ask you one more favor."

"I—"

"You need a ghost, right?"

"But—"

"Please. Take Richard. Try to help him move on like you did Sergei."

I wanted to just open the door and run out. "I—what am I supposed to do, break up with Czoltan and get back together with him to show Richard how it's done?"

"I don't know, but..." She wiped her eyes. "I loved him. And I think you must have too, at least a little. We owe it to him, even though he tried to kill us."

"That wasn't really him."

"No."

I turned over both possible answers in my head, not liking either of them. After a minute of silence, Desiree said, "Jae?"

"Look," I said. "I can't promise anything. But I'll try like hell to find a place for him, if it's not with me."

"Thank you so much." She wiped her face again, leaving the fur damp.

I pointed to her bedside table. "Tissues are your friend now. If you just wipe your face, everyone can see the wet fur."

"Thank you."

Her smile stayed with me out into the corridor, and that almost made the promise worth it.

Acknowledgments

This book was serialized on Patreon at patreon.com/kyellgold from March to December 2019. Thanks to all the patrons who supported this book there:

a stray cat
Ace Saber
Adept Omega
AJ
Allister Damien Gray
Anamosus
Arabian Darkstone
Ari Yena
Artur Silveira Fortes
Astro
Auren Drakeson
Avro Fox
Awkward Aeronaut
Ayven
Badger Furet
Baxley Toshi
Baylei
blargh
Brasen
Broadpaw Fox
Burley

buu38

CamTheMarten

Canis Rufus

Cardinalscissors

Cassandra Mann

caudamus

Chakai

Charles

Charlie Payne

Chris Paw

Christian Lopez

Clarke Macbeth

Crimson

ct030912

Dale Farmer

Dallas Bolen

Darwen

Dave B.

David Drollinger

del

Devyn Scott

Diego P

Dipper Rat

Dire

DJ Kyu

Dmitry P

Donovan Elk

Doug Kelly

Dunkelpfote

Echo Foxx

EgoSaber

Eliezer

Erik Johansson

erisil_lightarrow

Evey

Felrnn

Flann Moriath

FlatFootFox

Foxon Silverfur

Furiia

Furtastic Voss

Genisu Windpaw

Glassan

Grey

Gruffy

Ian Brandeberry

Injy

iqbunny

Jack Devries

Jakebe

Jarebear

Jasmine Smith

Jay1743

Jeremy C

Joey Watts

Joshua Owens

K H

Kairan Otter

Karmakat

Kato Okami

Kayod√© Lycaon

Kieran Gallagher

Kogawakenji

Korel Dagh

Kougo

kraosh

Kristi Bjerkaas
Kristofferson
Laimika
Laklen
Lazy Wolf
Leo
LethargicFox
Lumble
Makoh Dog
Malamutt
Malarwolfe
Malcolm F. Cross
Malec Wolgon
Marc Gold
Marcwolf
Martin Farley
Matt Wills
Matthew Ford
Mau
Max Pitbull
Michael
Mu Gamma
Multiroit
Nathan Hopp
NegaImage
Neil McIntosh
Nielas Sinclair
No name
Omegawolf Wildpaw
Oscar Landeros
oscar the sergal
Peri Llwyn
Phenris

Pinemarten Avatar

Poi Wong

Pootie Fang

ProwlingPaws

pwr

qazwsx7946

Rankine

Ratchet Fox

Redx Wolfski

Rei Loire

Remy Shep

repzzmonster

Ressy

Reyfar

Rhett

Risus

Riyo

RoflLion

Roger Gilson

Roman Ashley

Rooth

Ryan

Ryan McKown

Ryan Patrick Draa

sandcat

Shader

Shakal Draconis

Shane Elfield

ShironJackal

Silverfox 361

SilverS

Silwer

Sirberus Khaos

Skandranon Rashkae

Skeeter

Sketchy Wolf

SlyFox

SoarinPie

Spirit

Stoatmeal

Strawberry Puptart

SubtleSlight

sunkawakan

Tau Switchblade

Tidal wolf

Tiger

Tiller Brown

TomLeo

tone

Trent Grasse

Trevor Bygland

Trip

TuftTip

Tyfle

Tyler Brown

vagabonddiesel

Vaska

Vic

Viski

Vivian Burning

Will Cook (Midnight Hunter)

wolfeye

Wolfi

Yestin

Yifan Mai (Myf)

Yindi

Zachary Busto
zack

Thanks to Salt & Sage Books for their editorial help, to Brer and Alopex who published the original short story this was based on, to Dark End who encouraged me to write more of it. Thanks also to Ryan Campbell, David Cowan, Malcolm Cross, Watts Martin, and Melli Yoon for their help in making this book better.

As always, thanks to Mark and Grant and Buck at Argyll for their confidence and assistance. And my family, Mark, Jack, and Kobalt, for being there for me always.

ABOUT THE AUTHOR

Tim Susman started a novel in college and didn't finish one until almost twenty years later. In that time, he earned a degree in Zoology, worked with Jane Goodall, co-founded Sofawolf Press, and moved to California. He has attended Clarion in 2011 (arooo to my Narwolves!) and published short stories in Apex, Lightspeed, and ROAR, among others. Under the name Kyell Gold, he has published multiple novels and won several awards for his furry fiction. You can find out more about his stories at *timsusman.wordpress.com* and *www. kyellgold.com* and follow him on Twitter at @WriterFox.

ALSO BY TIM SUSMAN

If you would like to get monthly updates on upcoming publications, excerpts of works in progress, and writing tips, sign up for his mailing list at *http://kyellgold.substack.com*.

New Tibet

Breaking The Ice: Stories from New Tibet (editor) - On a hostile ice planet, survival is guaranteed to nobody.

Shadows in Snow (editor) - More stories from the unforgiving ice world of New Tibet.

Common and Precious - A kidnapped heiress comes to sympathize with her desperate captors, while her father discovers the limits of his power in trying to rescue her.

The Calatians

Book 1: The Tower and the Fox - Kip and his friends encounter prejudice and mysteries in their first few months at Prince George's College of Sorcery.

Book 2: The Demon and the Fox - The forces of revolution grow in Massachusetts as Kip and his friends rush to solve the mystery of the attack on the College of Sorcery.

Book 3: The War and the Fox - Kip and his friends are drafted into the fight for independence from Britain, but there is more at stake.

Book 4: The Revolution and the Fox - Two years after the war, Kip and his friends face their greatest threat yet.

Other books

The Price of Thorns - A down-on-his-luck thief meets the actual evil queen from many fairy tales when she offers him the job of a lifetime. (Coming 2022)

Writing as Kyell Gold:

Love Match

Love Match (vol. 1, 2008-2010) — Rocky arrives in the States from Africa and navigates the treacherous worlds of professional tennis and high school.

Love Match (vol. 2, 2010-2012) — Rocky begins his professional career, at the cost of his family and romantic relationships.

Love Match (vol. 3, 2013-2015) — As his career trends upward, Rocky's romantic life becomes less stable.

Out of Position (Dev and Lee)

Out of Position – Dev the football player and Lee the gay activist discover how to navigate their relationship. *(mature readers)*

Isolation Play – The continuing story of Dev and Lee, as they contend with family and friends in their search for acceptance. *(mature readers)*

Divisions – As Dev's team fights to make the playoffs, Lee fights to keep his sense of self. *(mature readers)*

Uncovered – The playoffs are here, and Dev needs his focus more than ever. So when Lee becomes too distracting, something has to give. *(mature readers)*

Over Time – Dev and Lee try to plan their future while dealing with crises all around them. *(mature readers)*

Ty Game — Dev's teammate Ty navigates an arranged marriage while also falling in love. *(mature readers)*

Tales of the Firebirds — A collection of stories exploring the lives of some of the other characters from the Out of Position series. *(mature readers)*

Titles – In the two weeks leading up to Dev's third try at a championship, Dev and Lee face new challenges and changes in their lives. *(mature readers)*

Dangerous Spirits

Green Fairy – A gay high school senior struggling through his final year finds a strange old book that changes his dreams and his life.

Red Devil – A gay fox who fled his abusive family in Siberia seeks help from a ghost who demands he give up his gay lifestyle.

Black Angel – A young otter struggles to understand her sexuality as her friends prepare for post-high school life and dreams of women in other times plague her.

Argaea

Volle – The story of how Volle came to Tephos, a spy masquerading as a noble, and the first adventure he had there. *(mature readers)*

The Prisoner's Release and Other Stories – The story of how Volle escaped from prison, and the story of what happened after, plus two other stories following characters from "Volle." *(mature readers)*

Pendant of Fortune – Volle returns to Tephos to defend his honor, but soon finds himself fighting for much more. *(mature readers)*

Shadow of the Father – Volle's son, Yilon, must travel to the far-off land he is meant to rule, but he will have to fight treachery to take the lordship. *(mature readers)*

Weasel Presents – Five short stories from the land of Argaea, including "Helfer's Busy Day" and "Yilon's Journal." *(mature readers)*

Return From Divalia — Years after a night of adventure ruined his life, a young wolf gets a chance at redemption. *(mature readers, coming 2022)*

Forester Universe

Waterways – The full story of Kory's journey to understand himself and what it means to be gay. *(mature readers)*

Bridges – Hayward seems content to set up pairs of his friends. But what does he really need for himself? *(mature readers)*

Science Friction – Vaxy never took sex seriously, until he found out the professor he was sleeping with was married... *(mature readers)*

Winter Games – Sierra Snowpaw was an unsure high school student when someone he thought was a friend changed his life. Now he's fifteen years older and still looking for answers. *(mature readers)*

The Mysterious Affair of Giles – A servant in a British manor house tries to solve a murder.

Dude, Where's My Fox? – Lonnie chases down a fox he hooked up with at a party as a way to get over his breakup. *(mature readers)*

Dude, Where's My Pack? — Lonnie tries to navigate relationships old and new. *(mature readers)*

Losing My Religion – On tour with his R.E.M. cover band, Jackson mentors the new guy in the band as his own life falls apart. *(mature readers)*

The Time He Desires — A Muslim immigrant struggles with the betrayal of his son and the dissolution of his marriage, as well as his own long-past trauma.

Camouflage — When Danilo is sent 500 years into the past, he must choose between safety in an unfamiliar world and his own sense of what is right. *(mature readers)*

Other Books

The Silver Circle – Valerie thought the old hunter was crazy when he warned her about werewolves—until she met one.

In the Doghouse of Justice – Seven stories of superheroes and their not-so-super relationships. *(mature readers)*

Twelve Sides — Twelve short stories about side characters from the above books. *(mature readers)*

Do You Need Help? — Writing advice for furry (and non-furry) writers.